JOE

LEGEND
OF THE

PHOENIX
RESURGENCE

LEGEND

OF THE

PHOENIX

RESURGENCE

A litRPG Adventure

Eternal Grind Book. I

Joel Poe

CONTENTS

Prologue

A thunderous rumble echoed through the high forest of Aelloria, disrupting the harmony of the woodland. Towering ancient trees swayed, their roots deeply seated in the earth as though they were the audience to an epic saga unfolding. The saga of a young blacksmith with a burning desire in his heart - a desire to protect, to defend, to conquer.

Joren stood in a clearing, his olive skin glistening with sweat and eyes aflame with determination. His muscular build was a testimony to his blacksmith roots and years of harsh training, his dark hair ruffled and untamed. His grip on the sturdy warhammer was unyielding, the weapon almost part of him. An interface visible only to him glowed in his eyes, the corner of his vision indicating his dwindling health and mana points, his current in game low level juxtaposed with that of his adversary's level 25.

The blue Ogre, a formidable creature towering over him, snarled, its eyes glowing ominously in the dwindling twilight. It lunged towards Joren, swinging a colossal arm in an attempt to swat him away. With an agile roll, Joren barely dodged the attack, feeling the rush of wind as the monstrous limb passed over his head. His health points, displayed in vibrant green on his HUD, took a hit.

"Flaming strike," Joren called out, focusing his dwindling mana into his warhammer. His weapon ignited in response, dancing flames wreathing the head of the hammer, mirroring the fire in his eyes. With a grit of his teeth, he watched as his mana points drained to a dangerous low, leaving a fine thread of blue on the bar.

Joren's heart pounded against his chest, his body acting on its own accord as years of training kicked in. He was more than a blacksmith now; he was a warrior. An image of the Ogre's vital points flashed on his interface, a product of his system's enemy analysis. It was risky, but it was a chance he had to take.

With a roar, he leapt towards the blue Ogre. His flame-wrapped warhammer swung in a fiery arc and met the monster's ribcage. The impact resonated throughout the forest, and a monstrous cry echoed, followed by the sizzling sound of burning flesh. The ogre wavered, blood spewing out, the green bar of its health points rapidly decreasing.

Joren didn't give it a chance to recover. With a shout, he brought his warhammer around one last time, directly aimed at the creature's head. The final swing was like the death knell, the air almost shuddering at the inevitability of the end.

The ogre's head exploded in a grotesque shower of blood and gore, a final roar echoing before it fell to the ground with a ground-shaking thud, its life extinguished. The victorious cry of a blacksmith-turned-warrior echoed through the forest.

● ●

Training Module
Ending Simulation in 3...2...1...

Custom Match Disengaged

● ●

1

A Blacksmith's Duty

The forge glowed with the flames that raged beneath the blacksmith's hammer. Each time Joren's tool came down, his heart beat just as hard. Forging weapons had become his full-time trade. There was never a slow season, as the village desperately needed the protection that his magical creations could provide.

Joren paused to scan his stock of soal stones—he was too low. With a swing of his hammer, he cursed the supplier who'd failed to deliver his shipment for the last fortnight.

Without soal stones, the weapons were merely hunks of metal—useless against the monsters that attacked Hopegrove. The night prior, his village had lost its best warrior to a giant spider. Its web loomed above the farmers' crops, and it wasn't rare to hear about a child that had disappeared during the day. One only had to look up at the lump of silk that dangled in the air to know where they'd gone.

Joren set aside his tool so that he could quench the broadsword in the clean water beside his station. He lifted the weapon toward the lamp overhead, so he could examine its condition—perfect. Still, he wanted to be positive that the weapon was crafted exactly as he wanted it to be.

Setting the sword aside, the young blacksmith uncorked a vial of lavender oil and poured it into the inspection bowl. He grabbed a soal stone and used a knife to shave a corner of its essence into the same bowl. While he mixed the ingredients, a light began to glow until a purple sunbeam burst from the mixture. Satisfied, Joren placed the sword's blade within the rays, turning it from side to side. The light changed from lavender to scarlet.

The blacksmith smiled, satisfied that the magic approved of his work. The light slowly faded, until only a cup of oil remained. He took the cup and gazed into its depths, wondering if he could find any trace of the soal stone's shavings. Instead, he found his reflection.

Joren was often surprised at his appearance because he didn't feel as young as he looked. A mere 17 years of life did not seem sufficient for all the turmoil he'd experienced. His unkempt brown hair should have been gray, and his smooth ivory skin should have been wrinkled. Other than the occasional burn scar, he looked like an ordinary young man.

Joren's brows wrinkled in frustration while he poured the lavender oil back into the vial, saving every last drop that he could—it wasn't a cheap ingredient to keep around. However, he wanted the comfort of knowing that his work would serve the community well. Joren was the only affordable blacksmith around, after all. They would be defenseless without his quality weapons. For this reason, the young blacksmith felt it was his duty to continue the work, as much as he wished to be elsewhere. The invented scenarios that magic provided him were simply not enough to quench his desire for more. However, he didn't have enough soal stones to power his gaming system, which was his only means of escape from reality. Without magic, the system was merely a combination of metal and coal.

Instead of setting the weapon aside with the rest of the orders, he took the broadsword outside. The sun was setting, so no one would be around to see him practicing. Joren inhaled, appreciating the fresh air that eluded him while working in the forge. The airships in the distance hovered a little lower than usual, their steam-powered engines filling the sky with smoke.

Joren stepped forward, charging an imaginary opponent. The sword's hilt was formed around a particularly sturdy soal stone. He'd been thrilled to discover it during his last delivery. It was black, mimicking onyx, yet it glowed crimson when it was activated. The weapon's strength, speed, and intuition grew with every movement. It was a beautiful sword, one that would serve a warrior well in the near future.

The blacksmith was able to pretend that *he* was that warrior, so long as he didn't put down the weapon. If he didn't stop fighting the invisible monster or strange enemy, he could exist in the fantasy. However, luck was not on Joren's side.

"Are you planning to put down your hammer, after all?"

Joren spun, facing the entrance to his forge. Thaddeus leaned against the doorway, a cigar in his mouth. It wasn't yet lit, but the blacksmith cursed himself for failing to notice him anyway. "You know that I can't," Joren answered. The man had visited Joren many times before, acting as a liaison between the blacksmith and the supplier. However, Joren noticed that something was wrong immediately. "Where's my shipment? It was due days ago."

Thaddeus took his sweet time removing a match from his front pocket and swiping it against the smithy's door frame. The smoke that leaked from his cigar filled the air with a bitter smell. Joren thought that he might as well have smoked coal instead. The man looked over the blacksmith's sword, which he refused to lower. "You're a talented kid, I'll give you that. It's too bad that the world doesn't treat talent kindly."

Joren sighed, walking over to the doorway so that he could lean the sword against the wall. He kept his distance, knowing that he couldn't trust Thaddeus—he worked for his competition, after all. "Where's my shipment?" Joren asked again. He needed soal stones to complete his work, and if he didn't provide weapons, then his village would disappear from history.

"Bad news, kid." Thaddeus exhaled a few rings of smoke before continuing, "The Ossein Guild raised their prices."

Joren leaned forward. "How much?"

Thaddeus laughed. "More than you can afford." The man looked the blacksmith up and down, inspecting the dirty rags that Joren used for clothing. Meeting Joren's eye again, he said, "It's time to put down the tools, kid. You can't compete with a big guild like Ossein." He motioned toward the open doorway that led to the forge. "I'll even buy back the rest of your soal supply."

Joren refused to believe that all his hard work had been for nothing—that the village that'd taken him in as a child was going to perish because of a guild's greed. "How much?" the blacksmith demanded.

Thaddeus moved toward Joren, faster than the blacksmith had ever thought he was capable of. He was thrown against the wall, the man's hand around his throat. "This isn't a game you can win, kid. It doesn't matter how much money you manage to scrape up from the muck in this doomed village. The Ossein Guild isn't going to sell you the materials anymore. They have their own blacksmiths—men that do what they're told when they're told."

"Hopegrove will die without soal-powered weapons," Joren stated. He refused to look away from the man, even when Thaddeus's hand tightened around his throat.

"You don't seem to get it, do you?" Thaddeus's cigar

glowed brightly, the sun disappearing over the horizon. The smoke kept Joren from inhaling any clean air.

The man reached for the newly-forged weapon only to find that its blade was pressed against his stomach. "You're the one who doesn't get it," Joren wheezed, gripping the sword's hilt tight.

Thaddeus released the blacksmith and backed away slowly, never removing his eyes from Joren's. "I'm trying to save your life, kid."

"You could have fooled me, old man." Joren raised the weapon and said, "If you're not going to help defend this village, then get out. I'll do it myself."

The man removed the cigar from his mouth for the first time since he arrived. "How are you going to do that? Ossein owns all of the soal and coal mines in the realm. If you were smart, you'd leave this filthy place and head to the city. At least you'd have protection there." Ash fell from Thaddeus's cigar, and the flame disappeared.

"If *you* were smart, you'd leave right now." Joren raised the sword, activating the crimson soal stone. The magic could be felt by both of them, but only one had control of it.

"Don't say that I didn't warn you, kid." Thaddeus flicked

his cigar to the ground, stamping out the remaining smoke. He was gone in the next breath that Joren took.

Panicking, Joren retreated into his forge and locked the steel door behind him. He dropped the sword and ran his hands roughly through his tangled hair. Joren knew that Ossein was growing in power. They had either recruited or threatened the other blacksmiths, extinguishing their businesses. The once-thriving coal town of Hopegrove declined when Ossein took over their mines. Without a stable income, the town had withered away. The remaining citizens couldn't afford to leave the little land that they had. Families were already struggling to eat, and the only thing that Joren could offer them was affordable weapons to protect themselves with.

The blacksmith threw his fist into the wall, unable to do anything other than curse Ossein and the power that they'd amassed. He drew his hand back and stared at his shaking fingers—a bruise was forming around his knuckles. "What do I do?" Joren asked himself. He was alone in the forge other than the weapons that he'd made with his own two hands. They were silent in response to his question, but he could still feel the magic pulsing through the room.

Afraid of what Thaddeus would do, he grabbed his last box of soal stones and hid them beneath the floor along with his most valuable weapons. Before he closed the latch, he grabbed a stone and placed it beside his hammer. He stared at the tool for a long time before sliding the table back into place, disguising the secret compartment he'd built into the flooring.

It wasn't long before Joren fed the furnace and began his work. The young blacksmith was a creative and determined person. It was one of the reasons he was so beloved by the village folk. He could design weapons within moments, and recreate the concept with ease. All it took was imagination, manual labor, and materials— materials that he *would* obtain. It didn't matter to Joren that Ossein refused to sell to him and threatened his life if he continued to forge. Nothing was going to stop him from protecting those he cared about.

Ossein had taken over the mines, but some mines had been abandoned. If Joren was going to find soal stones on his own, that was where they'd be. He would need to leave in the dead of night so the guild wouldn't see him. Joren would have to be quick. He needed the right tool for the job, as well as a weapon that would protect him against the creatures that roamed the forest. There was only one thing that he would trust to get him through this difficult task— his hammer.

The heat from the furnace made Joren sweat, but he didn't break focus as he reshaped his hammer into a formidable weapon. He sharpened one side so that he would be able to dig through the mine's rock. He added weight to the hammer's flat end. Lastly, the stone was welded into the hilt. The soal's magic pierced the weapon's core, becoming one with the new creation.

Joren swung the war hammer, adjusting to the new weight. It required two hands to wield, but it felt right in his grip. Finally, he donned his darkest cloak, hiding the weapon beneath the fabric. He exited the forge, securing the door behind him. The three moons hovered in the sky, each one in a different stage of waning.

Although the night was full of monsters and enemies, Joren walked into the forest with his head held high. He would return to his village as their savior—at least, that's what Joren hoped.

2

A Guild's Mine

Joren avoided the crop fields so that he wouldn't have to walk under the giant webs hovering above them. It was going to be difficult to evade trouble traveling through the forest, but the young blacksmith had become accustomed to the creatures that roamed his world.

He was prepared for an attack, his senses on high alert while he tiptoed across a piranhas' creek. A small bridge had been built over the running water, but the little devils were smart, lying in wait beneath the rotting wood. One sound from the aging path and a deadly bite would pierce the traveler's skin.

Joren had found a less-traveled path downstream, so he was able to avoid such an encounter. Once he'd crossed, the young man looked back and saw glowing eyes staring back at him from the water—he was lucky. Sweat dripped down his spine when he heard the sopping wet steps that came from a slime beast. Their bodies were born from the decay of corpses. If they had the chance to grab him, then the blacksmith would have been absorbed into their mass of muck. The size of the slime beast equaled the number of victims it had taken.

Joren waited until the squishy steps had faded into the distance before continuing his journey. The trek was longer than it had to be, but he wanted to survive this quest. Without him, his people would be defenseless. The mine's entrance yawned open like a digesting snake. There were no Ossein guards around to block his path, but it would only be a matter of time before their rounds led them to the mine.

Hidden from view within the darkness of the cavern, Joren reached into his pocket and revealed a small metal orb. He'd prepped the contraption by filling it with soal powder. He shook the orb, humming under his breath until the orb was hovering over his palm. It rose high above the blacksmith, and by the time it reached the mine's support beams, it was glowing with a warm light. The light followed him as he moved forward, attracted to the hand that had awakened it.

Joren concentrated on the path ahead, noting every dark crevice in the mine. Although it was abandoned, that didn't mean the monsters hadn't taken up residence. The tracks beneath his feet were rusted and misshapen. It was hard to determine if the abuse was from wear over time or if something monstrous had crushed the metal under its weight.

The surface was gutted, so much so that a shaft was built. The Ossein Guild had dug deep underground, stopping only once the scarce findings weren't making them a profit anymore. However, Joren had to try anyway. It was nearly impossible to steal from an active mine, as they'd be guarding it with more care.

The blacksmith tripped over some loose rubble.

A snort reverberated through the cavern. Joren stopped midstep and peered into the tunnel on his right. With a small motion of his hand, the light veered toward the noise. Once he saw the silhouette of the large sleeping troll, he beckoned the light back to him, dimming its brilliance until it was but a speck in the darkness.

Joren gripped his hammer tight. Silently, he moved forward, wincing when he saw the mine cage's condition ahead. Rusted metal and worn rope were the last things he needed when silence was his key to survival.

The blacksmith stepped onto the lift, testing its integrity. The metal cringed under his weight, but Joren had considered this problem before leaving the smithy. He pulled out a small vial from his cloak pocket and poured the contents into the crevices of the mechanism, hoping that the whale oil would do its job.

Joren tensed when he pulled the lever that would lower him farther into the mine. After a few questionable creaks, he allowed himself to exhale. The light followed Joren down, as silent as the old lift.

When the young man reached the bottom, he cursed, startled by the rock gremlins crawling at his feet. His hammer came down on the tops of their heads, shattering their forms in a matter of moments. They weren't threatening alone, but if they'd decided to band together he could have been crushed beneath their combined weight.

One of them managed to bite his calf. "Little bastard," Joren cursed while knocking the nuisance aside. However, it wasn't long before he reached the end of the tunnel.

Admiring his newly-forged hammer, he said, "Let's get to work." He used the sharpened end of his weapon to pick at the rock wall in front of him.

Every once in a while, a chunk of dark rock would tumble to his feet. He rubbed the black coating in hopes that a soal stone would reveal itself, but it was only ever coal. He tossed the coal aside and kept digging.

Hours passed without Joren finding a single soal stone. The orb flickered above, telling him that it was running low on soal powder. "Damn it," he spat. The sun would be rising within the hour, which meant that the guards were likely to spot him at the entrance. Sighing, Joren stared at the wall. His grip on the hammer tightened. "Just a little more." It only took three more swings before the steel tool clanged against something harder than coal. The blacksmith smiled, his heart pounding in anticipation.

Desperately digging around the discovery with his fingers, he used the hammer's edge to scrape and pry at the dark rock. Finally, he held it in his hands. It was heavier than any soal stone that he'd come across before. Carefully, he tapped the stone with his hammer. The dark coating fell apart, revealing metal. Joren was confused, but he continued to clean the object anyway. "What is—"

He didn't have a chance to finish his question before the

metal awoke with vengeance. His skin burned, but he couldn't remove it from his flesh. It had seared into his hand. As much as he tried to fight it, Joren let out a scream of anguish.

The heat was nothing like he'd experienced before, even in his forge. The blacksmith's hand burned, but the flames weren't contained to his hand. The pain traveled up his arm, through his shoulder, until it coursed through his veins. His skin glowed with saffron light. Overwhelmed, Joren fell to his knees, desperate to remove the object from his body.

The metal spread up his arm, no matter how hard he clawed at his own skin. It was only when the fire in his veins began to cool that Joren could comprehend what he was staring at. The object was silver beneath the heat. It was once a small diamond-shaped hunk of metal that had fit into the palm of his hand, but it had grown in size. The strange item covered Joren's entire forearm.

Swirling symbols were engraved on its surface, and writing started to rise from the metal. The floating symbols were incomprehensible. The ache that the intense heat had left behind was forgotten when Joren realized that the words were morphing into something that he could understand. "What are you?" he asked the foreign metal.

There was no voice to be heard, but the words solidified in the air, providing him with an answer.

Fire Class Artifact

"An artifact?" Joren looked to the spot where he'd found the item. There was nothing else that he could see. The blacksmith guessed that it must have been an old invention from how deep it was embedded into the earth. Though, he'd never seen one as unique as the one in his arm.

Joren stood, ignoring the wobble in his knees as he did so. The words faded from his view, so he shook his arm in an attempt to bring them back. Instead, he felt intense heat grow in his hand. He stopped, waiting for the pain to come—it didn't.

Cautiously, he moved his arm up and down. The heat increased, but it remained in his palm rather than spreading throughout his body. Joren grabbed his hammer in hopes of extinguishing the flames, but they only spread into the weapon. The soal stone embedded in its hilt ignited as if it was the sun.

Although the blacksmith was wary of the flames, he continued to hold on tight to his hammer. Words formed in the air again.

Level 2 War Hammer

"Level 2?" As soon as he uttered the question, a roar sounded from above. "Oh no," Joren whispered into the darkness. The flames died along with his curiosity. The blacksmith had woken the troll, which meant that he was trapped in the mine. His stomach dropped, leaving behind a sense of dread.

Joren threw the hood of his cloak over his head and summoned the orb into his free palm. Adrenaline made his heart pump fast, allowing him to hold the hammer comfortably in one hand. The rock gremlins fled at the sound of the troll above them. The lift shook with each step that the monster took. It was looking for the source of the noise, which meant it was likely near the mine shaft— right where he would appear on the surface.

Without any other choice, Joren stepped onto the lift and pulled the lever. The oil had lubricated the contraption, so it didn't squeal. It was a small comfort while the blacksmith prepared to face the deadly beast on the ground level. He had failed to obtain soal stones for his weapons, but he'd found something else. He hoped to trade the ancient object for what the village needed.

Joren pondered which trader he would approach first as he drew closer to the surface. He didn't want to acknowledge the fact that he might perish the moment he stepped off of the lift. The orb flickered one last time before fading completely. He was left in total darkness as he stepped onto the surface. Joren pressed flat against the mine's wall. Listening, he could hear the troll's breath. The monster had heard the lift but it was as blind as Joren was in the dark cavern. The only thing that the blacksmith could do was quietly inch his way up the tunnel, recalling the path he'd taken before.

The troll took two giant steps in Joren's direction, and the young man panicked. He bolted forward, uncaring of the noise he made, to avoid being crushed. However, it wasn't the noise that gave him away, it was the flames that burst from both of his hands. He dropped his hammer, expecting the fire to burn him. He didn't have enough time to contemplate the cool flames licking his palms. He looked up at the troll which stood as tall as the tunnel's support beams. The creature had to bend down so that it wouldn't hit its head on the ceiling.

Joren had seen trolls roaming the edges of the forest many times before, but never had he imagined that it would be so ugly. He had the once-in-a-lifetime opportunity to admire the sickly-green skin, stinking rolls of belly fat, and putrid breath that encircled Joren's puny body. The blacksmith wished that he'd never had the chance to do so. Especially when the troll leaned down to swipe at him with its overly-muscled arm.

Joren dove to the side and away from his weapon. He cursed when he landed on his backside, but that was the moment he saw the words hovering above the troll.

Level 2 Troll

3/3 Health

Panicked, Joren quickly glanced at the words hovering above his own head. They could've been seen even without the light that emanated from his fists.

Level 1 Warrior

The words stabilized when he acknowledged them. Sadly, he had a lower level than the troll, which made him realize how utterly screwed he was.

Trolls weren't clever by any means, but they could move fast. Joren only had time to take a breath before the monster lunged at him again. The blacksmith dove between the monstrous legs in front of him, taking the opportunity to hit the troll's kneecap on his way through.

Joren didn't expect his hit to make an impact, but the monster roared in pain. Looking back, the young man caught a glimpse of the burn mark that was seared into the monster's flesh. More words formed in front of him, disappearing as fast as they came.

Critical Hit From Fire Fist

2/3 Health Remains

Realizing the opportunity he was given, Joren ran for his war hammer. Its level remained the same as before, the information floating above the weapon. The blacksmith's flames blazed when they touched the Level 2 hammer. The soal stone within the weapon only added to the power that coursed up his arms.

The troll couldn't stand on its damaged knee, but it turned to lunge at Joren again. Except the blacksmith was ready with a defense. He blocked the monstrous arm with a swing of his hammer. The arm flew aside, allowing Joren a chance to bring the hammer down on the creature's chest.

Critical Hit From War Hammer

1/3 Health Remains

The troll grabbed onto Joren's hammer, holding it hostage. Allowing instinct to take control of his body, the young blacksmith brought his flaming fist back. With as much strength as he could muster, he sent the flames into the troll's chin.

Critical Hit From Flaming Uppercut

Level 2 Troll Defeated

5 Experience Points Gained

You Leveled Up!

The words popped up one by one, nearly causing Joren to fall backward in confusion. However, he held his ground. The troll collapsed onto its back—dead.

Breathing was difficult as Joren ran from the corpse he'd left behind. He didn't know how he'd defeated the monster with only three hits. He didn't know why the necessary information he needed revealed itself to him. All he *did* know was that the sun had risen, and he needed to get back to his forge before he was cau—

"I knew you'd try to pull something, kid." Thaddeus's voice echoed down the mine. The man blocked Joren's escape at the entrance. The worst part? He wasn't alone.

3

An Artifact's Voice

"What are you doing here?" Joren asked Thaddeus. The blacksmith discreetly sized up the Ossein Guards—they were large, armored, and each one held a weapon in their hand. Joren's hammer felt inadequate in comparison to the obstacles in front of him.

"I'd ask you the same thing, but I think I already know," Thaddeus replied. He motioned to Joren's weapon. "You're talented, kid. I've never seen a hammer quite like that one."

"You've mentioned my talent before. If you enjoy my work so much, why don't you let me leave? I didn't find any soal stones. You don't have to worry about theft." Joren backed up slowly, inching his way into the darkness of the mine.

Thaddeus shook his head slowly. "It doesn't matter. You trespassed and openly defied the guild. Our master doesn't let behavior like that slide." The guards stepped forward as one unit, trained in offensive attacks. The words hovering above their heads caused a shiver to crawl down the blacksmith's spine.

Level 5 Ossein Guard

Level 7 Ossein Guard

Level 10 Ossein Guard

Thaddeus allowed the guards to lead the charge, but Joren could still see his level floating under the sun's rays.

Level 40 Thief

Joren could see the sun peeking through the trees behind the guards, but there wasn't a slice of space for him to run between them. His one hope was to retreat into the mine and hide. The young blacksmith only took a step before a broken female voice sounded in the cavern. *"Jo-ren."*

He looked back and forth, searching for the source. Joren's opponents advanced, unbothered by the mysterious voice. Survival was the blacksmith's top priority, so he turned and ran into the mine, hoping that the troll was truly dead.

"According to my calculations, Molten Hammer will have a 90% success rate against the Ossein Guards."

Startled, Joren leaped to the side, expecting a woman to be running beside him. Finding nothing but the guards on his tail, he said, "What is that?"

"Your Molten Hammer can be activated by throwing your weapon at the aggressors behind you." The woman's voice was as clear as the sound of the blacksmith's pounding heart.

Confused, he responded to the void, "I'm not throwing my hammer at them! I'll lose my only defense."

"Sacrificing your defense to lay a trap gives you an 80% chance of escape. If you continue on your current course, your chance of survival is 10%. My calculations are never wrong." The woman's voice was devoid of emotion. She wasn't scared of the guards or angry at the blacksmith. She was simply providing information.

"A trap? Are you crazy?" Joren shouted, his breath coming fast in the darkness. However, he didn't slow his speed—he could still hear the guards behind him.

"Your chances of success have increased to 95% with the cover of darkness. Throw your weapon, Joren. I'll activate Molten Hammer for you."

The war hammer that Joren gripped tightly in his hands lit with fire. He wasn't as startled by it as before, but this time, the flames burned. "Shit!" Joren dropped the weapon, stopping in his tracks.

"Throw your hammer in three... two... one..."

Without another choice, Joren gave in and picked up the scorching weapon. The flames from the hammer provided him with enough light that he could aim. The war hammer landed in the middle of the three guards. Upon impact, the weapon dissolved into molten liquid. The metal splattered against his opponents, burning them where they stood. The lava rose high enough to submerge their knees. When they tried to run, the liquid hardened, trapping them.

Molten Hammer Successful

The words that materialized before Joren disappeared as quickly as they'd formed. The guards continued to scream in pain. However, Thaddeus had avoided the attack. He stared hard at Joren, the glow from the lava dimming as the moments passed. The man's face was contorted into an expression of surprise and excitement.

Dread filled Joren's chest as he watched Thaddeus turn and run toward the exit.

"Well done—Joren. You've evaded capture. With more— training, you'll be able to activate Molten Hammer on— your own." The woman's speech was broken as she praised the blacksmith. Words came and went until the voice in Joren's head disappeared altogether.

The Ossein Guards were in too much pain to stay conscious. Even though Joren was sad to have lost his hammer, he was grateful for the sacrifice when he left the mine and stepped into the sunshine.

Thaddeus was nowhere to be seen, which made Joren nervous. He wondered if the so-called thief had gone to gather more reinforcements. If so, Joren knew where his next stop would be.

Joren's muscles ached from mining for soal and fighting with a troll. Still, he ran through the forest, desperate for sanctuary. His arm was heavy from the metal that had been embedded in his skin. The blacksmith pulled at the artifact as he fled. Joren thought that if he managed to remove it, then he could leave for the city to find a buyer. He wondered if that would be long enough for Thaddeus to forget about him. More importantly, he could return to the village with enough soal stones to stock their armory.

A wet grumble sounded in the forest, and it took Joren too long to realize that he'd stumbled across a slime beast. He wasn't sure if it was the same one he hid from the previous night, but it was just as terrifying.

"No, I'm so close," Joren whispered to himself. The beast blocked his path across the creek. Through the gaps in the monster's dripping muck of a body, he could see the piranhas' eyes staring up at him.

Level 1 Poison Piranha

At least a dozen titles popped up from the water's surface. The slime beast turned its head, curious about Joren.

Level 2 Slime Beast

Health 2/2

As frightened as Joren was, he took the time to examine the words that floated in the air. There was other information besides titles and health levels. A small button floated just outside of his vision. The more he concentrated on it, the clearer it became.

Menu

"Are you serious? What the hell is this thing?" Joren shouted, shaking his arm in frustration. The slime beast took that as a challenge and rose up on its squishy legs. "Hey lady, where are you? The time to help is now!" the blacksmith called out.

There was no response from the mysterious voice.

"Lady! Help!" Joren held his ground, knowing there was no way he could outrun the creature. The monster dove forward, and the blacksmith imagined what it would be like to be absorbed into its disgusting mass—it wasn't a good image.

Burning Roundhouse Unlocked

There was no voice to guide Joren, but the words appeared before his eyes. Just as they dissipated into thin air, instinct took over his body. With strength and precision, the ordinary blacksmith drew his right leg back and launched the limb forward. Flames burst from Joren's foot as he did so, striking the beast in its only solid body part— the heart. The slime beast flew backward and landed in the water.

Critical Hit From Burning Roundhouse

1/2 Health Remains

The flames that burned the heart were extinguished, but they no longer mattered. The piranhas took the opportunity to swarm the beast, consuming its oily flesh. Joren didn't stop to watch as he jumped over the creek and sprinted out of the forest.

0/2 Health Remains

Level 2 Slime Beast Defeated

1 Experience Point Earned

"I don't care!" Joren shouted, flailing his arms in an attempt to rid himself of the information that kept popping up in front of him. Entering the village, the passersby stared at the blacksmith as if he'd lost his mind. He knew he had to hide if he wanted to live another day. The forge was no longer safe, so there was only one place he had left.

Joren knocked on the steel door that guarded his childhood home. Marylynn greeted the blacksmith with flour and a smile on her face. "My dear boy, it's been ages since you've visited." For a moment, Joren couldn't respond. The title above his foster mother's head warmed his heart and caused worry to pool in his bowels.

Rare Household Member

Health 1/1

Stuttering over his words, he said, "Sorry, I've been busy with orders. Will you feed me anyway?" Joren leaned into the doorway, allowing the aroma to caress his nose. "Is that fresh bread?"

Marylynn laughed and said, "And leftover pigeon soup." The kind woman stepped aside for her adopted child. She didn't embrace him as normal family members often did, knowing that Joren wasn't the type to show affection.

"That sounds great." Joren missed catching pigeons for his foster parents. The little creatures were slow and very gullible. As a child, Joren would set traps for them behind the house because they were constantly trying to sneak into the walls for warmth.

"First, you need a bath." Marylynn sniffed Joren, confused. "Did the forge win? You reek of smoke."

Joren hid his face by turning toward the bathing area. "I was too tired to wash up last night."

"You've always worked too hard. It's okay to stop and smell the roses once in a while, my dear." Joren listened to Marylynn saunter into the kitchen before opening the door to the bathing area. He stepped into a small room full of copper pipes. His first earnings had gone toward improving his foster family's home. A bathing area was the least he could've offered them after they'd taken in an angry abandoned boy.

While feeding the small furnace coal from the bucket beside it, he turned levers until water poured from the faucet above the tub. Hot water was exactly what Joren needed, and he was willing to wait the several minutes it took for the pipes to warm up.

Before removing his soiled clothes, he asked the void, "Lady, can you hear me?" When no one answered, he sighed and made himself comfortable in the small tub. He didn't even care that the water was still freezing cold. It numbed the ache in his muscles and the bruises on his skin.

Joren closed his eyes, but it wasn't long before his curiosity got the best of him. He reached out to the floating button at the corner of his vision.

Menu

The word beckoned him as much as the hot water did. He needed to know what he'd found in the mine. More importantly, he needed to remove it. The blacksmith hoped that he would find the answer when he pressed his fingers onto the solidified word. The word didn't disappear as he'd feared it would; rather, a list formed directly in front of him.

Class

Experience

Skills

Weapons

Armor

Items

The Menu's choices were eerily similar to his gaming system at the forge. Soal stones and machinery combined allowed him to view a world filled with information. Most of the games he played would permit him to keep track of his avatar's health and levels. The blacksmith took every opportunity that he had to enter such realms, even if they weren't real. However, these weren't some random words scattered within a hologram. Joren took the time to explore each tab.

Class:

Warrior: Close combat abilities.

Perks: High health. Increased strength.

Weaknesses: Long-range attacks. Stealth.

Experience:

Current Level: 2

Current Experience Points Earned: 1

Experience Points Needed To Level Up: 6

Skills:

Current Skill Points: 1

Unlocked Skills:

Fire Fist: Sets fists ablaze with flames. Strength increase. High success rate.

Blazing Uppercut: Sets fists ablaze. Target lock. Medium success rate.

Molten Hammer: Lava application. Trapping capabilities. Medium success rate.

Burning Roundhouse: Sets feet ablaze. Strength increase. Speed increase. High success rate.

Locked Skills:

Data Not Found

Weapons:

War Hammer: Level 2. Reconstruction in progress.

Armor:

Cloak: Disguise. Inventory increase.

Chest Piece: Cotton Shirt.

Leg Armor: Leather Pants. Leather Boots.

Items:

Artifact: Technology. Origins unknown.

Soal Stone: Power generator.

Whale Oil: Lubricant.

Joren was unsettled to see all of his belongings listed on the Menu. That meant that the artifact that he'd found could record him—label him. The blacksmith pondered whether or not it was making him into something or showing him what he already was.

"Do you have any questions about your Menu, Joren?"

Startled, Joren leaped out of the tub and slipped on the concrete floor. He searched for his weapon, forgetting that he'd lost it in the mine. He stood, searching for the source of the voice again. "Where are you?" he demanded.

"I'm within you, Joren."

"What does that mean? Am I losing my mind?" he asked the void.

The woman's voice laughed, but it was without humor. *"Your health levels are high. There's no need to worry. I simply mean that you've activated me with your touch. Look at your right arm, Joren."*

Joren looked down at the artifact that had provided him with the means to escape the mine. "You're the artifact?" he asked. The blacksmith ran his fingers over the metallic surface. There were no scars from where it had seared into his body. It was a seamless transition from skin to metal.

"I am Fenria—an artificial intelligence that was programmed to guide you through your journey." Her voice softened. *"I imagine you have questions for me, Joren."*

Joren considered for a moment before responding. "How do I remove you?"

"My intended purpose is to lead you to the Inmost Cave. There, we can access the information that you seek." Her tone gave away nothing other than calculative information. Joren didn't trust the AI or the ones who had built her.

"Why didn't you respond to me earlier? I spoke to you," Joren challenged.

"My body is still uploading into your nervous system. You will be able to summon me at will when the upload is complete. Until then, I'll conserve power by shutting down for short periods of time."

"When will that happen?" Joren asked, nervous at the prospect of something foreign absorbing into his body without permission.

"It will only be complete when we reach the Inmost Cave. There, you will discover your purpose." Joren didn't like being told what to do, especially when it meant leaving his family. *"Step into the shower, Joren. Your body temperature is dropping."*

Unable to deny the shivers that plagued him, he stepped into the tub and let the water run over his cold skin. He stared at the artifact, watching the dirt tumble from its surface. "What powers you? Do you use soal stones?"

"I am powered by an Undying Flame. Soal stones are produced from the earth, but the flame is created by something much more powerful," Fenria explained.

Joren couldn't comprehend something more powerful than a soal stone, so he was skeptical when he asked, "And what made this *Undying Flame*?"

"I'm sorry, Joren. I don't have access to that information at this time. My current objective is to lead you to the Inmost Cave, as well as train you to use your skills."

"As comforting as that is, I'm going to pass. I'm sure there's something in my forge that will remove you." Joren cringed, knowing it was going to hurt. "Whatever you are, you'll fetch a good price in the city."

"I am not meant for anyone else, Joren. You alone can wield me." Fenria almost sounded offended, but the blacksmith chalked it up to his imagination.

"I'm sure that's what you're programmed to say. For all I know, you could be some ancient child's toy. Aelloria is an old realm, after all." Fenria didn't say anything more as Joren continued to cleanse himself of the long day and night. By the time he was done eating and tucked into his childhood bed, he had forgotten about Fenria's warning completely.

4

A Boy's Nightmare

Joren awoke to the sound of screams. He peered out of the window to find that night had fallen over the village. Before he could rise from his bed, Barnabas, his foster father, threw the door open. The steel frame cringed from the force. "Joren, we're being attacked."

The blacksmith threw on his clothes while he asked, "Monsters again?"

Barnabas paused before answering, "Yes, but it's never been this bad." Impatient, Joren's foster father picked up the blacksmith's cloak and wrapped it around his shoulders. It surprised Joren when Barnabas embraced the young man, holding him tight.

"We'll get through this like we always do, Barnabas," Joren assured. He didn't understand the fear in the man's eyes. The village was regularly attacked by creatures from the forest—they were a small pocket of people with very little protection.

Barnabas released Joren only to hand him a dagger. "Take

this. Go to the forge and gather as many weapons as you can. The guardians will need them."

Joren tried to give the weapon back. "I made this for you. You can't get by on your strength alone. What would Marylynn do without you?" Barnabas was a large man who prided himself on defense. He rarely used soal-powered weapons, as he delegated them to the weaker village folk.

Barnabas huffed. "Your mother is stronger than you think. Plus, you're the child. How would it look if I left you defenseless?" Joren's foster father tried to make light of the situation, causing a frown to appear on the young man's tired face. Still, he pocketed the dagger. "Marylynn is getting the children and elderly to safety. Find me when you get the weapons. I'll be at the fields."

Without another word, Barnabas departed the small home with a determined look in his eye. Joren listened to the cries of his village for only a moment more before he slipped out of the back entrance. "Fenria? Are you there?" he asked the void.

Joren picked up his speed after realizing that Fenria wasn't going to be of any help. He rounded the corner and scrutinized his forge. The door had been broken down, but he didn't see any movement inside. Taking a deep breath, he forced his shaking body to move forward.

The smithy had been turned upside down. His shelves, tools, and supplies had been ransacked. "But they didn't find you, did they?" Joren muttered to himself. He scooted the table out of his way to collect the hidden weapons from beneath the floor. The remainder of his soal stones, weapons, and armor were right where he'd left them. He laid them all out on the floor, searching for armor that would protect Barnabas.

"You're one dumb kid, aren't you?"

Joren stood and turned toward the entrance, withdrawing the dagger from his belt. "Why are you here? The village is being attacked. The least you could do is let me die in battle."

Thaddeus didn't have a cigar between his lips as he usually did. Joren could tell that the thief was struggling with its absence—he was fidgeting while he stared at the blacksmith. "That was the goal, but I'd rather not risk it."

"Am I really worth all this trouble? It's just some soal stones, and I didn't even find any. There's no reason to kill me." Joren shifted his feet ever so slightly, preparing for an attack.

Thaddeus chuckled. "This is so much bigger than some

lousy soal stones, kid."

"Joren, you must proceed with caution. The thief should not be underestimated." Fenria's words caused Joren to jump, which made Thaddeus smile.

"Is it true that the artifact can speak?" The thief eyed the embedded metal in Joren's arm. Joren instinctually covered the artifact and gripped the knife tighter.

"I don't know what you're talking about. This is an armor prototype. You know me—I like to experiment with materials when I have them." Joren's heart was pounding, and he could feel a burning building in his palms.

"It doesn't matter what you say, kid. I know what you have, and I've been hired to bring it to someone who can wield it properly." Thaddeus reached behind the doorframe and exposed a weapon.

Confused, Joren said, "How do you have that?"

"Like I said before, I enjoy your work. I had to see if the weapon was salvageable, yet it had reformed by the time I made it back to the mine. Peculiar, isn't it?" Thaddeus waved the hammer through the air with both hands, though his muscles were struggling with the weight.

"Why didn't you tell me that my hammer was okay?"

Joren asked Fenria under his breath.

"The war hammer's reconstruction was listed in the Menu, Joren."

Frustrated, the blacksmith said, "Thanks for returning my hammer. It's some of my best work." Joren glanced at the pile of soal-powered weapons on the floor, knowing he would have to use one in order to win against the hammer. The villagers' screams increased each moment that Joren spoke with the thief. The ground shook with the vibration of giant monster feet. He had to get rid of Thaddeus fast so that he could deliver the weapons. "Look, I'll give you the artifact. Just leave me and the village alone."

The artifact burned with heat, causing the dagger to burst into flames. The small soal stone within the knife glowed a bright orange. Thaddeus responded, "It doesn't look like it wants to leave, kid. If the stories are true, then it can only be removed when the host has died." Sighing, the thief continued, "Well, let's get this over with."

Thaddeus lunged at Joren, the hammer coming down hard where the blacksmith had been standing. The young man grabbed a sword as he leaped over the table. He needed to wait for the right moment to strike. The hammer was too heavy for Thaddeus, so he was slow.

"Don't make this any harder than it is, Joren. You can still die with dignity." Thaddeus prattled on as he chased Joren around the forge.

"Dignity? I don't think a thief has a right to lecture anyone about that," Joren said, hoping to anger Thaddeus to the point of sloppiness.

Thaddeus paused only a moment before he said, "What else has the artifact told you?"

"The thief's left side is vulnerable to attacks. Fire Fist has a 60% chance of success if you land a critical hit to his side." A red circle appeared before Joren, surrounding the exact area that he needed to attack. However, all Joren could concentrate on was Thaddeus's health level.

Health 4/4

"I don't have time to mess around, Fenria. Tell me how to bring him down *now*." Joren leaped from one corner of the room to the other, refusing to leave the weapons and armor vulnerable by escaping.

"Understood, Joren. I can unlock Rapid Fire, but you won't be able to use your abilities for several minutes afterward. If your blows don't land, you will be vulnerable to his attacks. Are you willing to move forward, Joren?"

Joren didn't take the time to consider the consequences when he said, "Do it!"

New Ability Unlocked: Rapid Fire

Joren locked in on the red circle that guided him to Thaddeus's side. With speed he'd never been capable of before, he rushed at his attacker, striking his left side multiple times.

Critical Hit From Rapid Fire

3/4 Health Remains

Joren's fists met the thief's flesh in continuous succession. The man's liver, ribs, gut, chest, and face were taking a lot of damage. Still, it took minutes to bring the thief down. The blacksmith was close to ending Thaddeus when the thief managed to push Joren aside and swing the hammer into the young man's chest.

"You've been critically damaged, Joren. Abandon Rapid Fire."

Rapid Fire Will End In 5 Seconds

The warning only pushed Joren further. "No way. People are counting on me." Despite the ache in the blacksmith's chest and the warning that Fenria kept repeating, he advanced again. "It's time for you to go, Thaddeus," he spat.

His fists burned with the flames that encompassed them, but he didn't slow his speed until Thaddeus had dropped the hammer and his health was on the brink of defeat.

1/4 Health Remains

Rapid Fire Will End In 0 Seconds

The flames died when Thaddeus fell to the ground. Joren's breathing was ragged, never before having moved so fast. His arms burned with fatigue, but he had accomplished his goal.

"The thief is unconscious. Now is the time to finish him, Joren. You will not need your abilities to complete the task." Despite Thaddeus's attempt on Joren's life, the blacksmith didn't move to end him. Instead, he loaded up the weapons and armor onto a cart. He made sure to stash some of the soal stones in his satchel and rested the war hammer over his shoulder. He even picked out some armor for himself, as he didn't want to lower his health levels any more than he had.

"When will he wake up, Fenria?" Joren asked.

"Rapid fire caused severe damage to his body. He will be

unconscious for at least 24 hours, Joren."

Joren nodded. "Good. Then we have time."

"You need to train before entering battle, Joren. The enemies ahead are not natural," Fenria stated.

"What does that mean? Monsters are bad, but they're natural to this realm just like humans." Joren couldn't help but scratch at the skin around the artifact. The cart cringed with every bump that he rolled it over. He worried that the noise would attract monsters, but it looked like the guardians had led the beasts away. The houses he passed had already been evacuated. Those who hadn't escaped were left behind, their corpses half-eaten or simply crushed.

Fenria continued, *"The monsters have already passed from this realm. Their motivation comes from another source."* Choosing to ignore Fenria, the blacksmith instead concentrated on dragging the cart through the mud. He climbed over several hills until he reached the fields just beyond the village. They were once used as crop fields, but the farmers had to find other ground when the man-eating moles built their tunnels beneath the soil two decades prior.

He hid behind a copse of trees, searching for Barnabas

amid all the chaos. It was when he saw the monsters up close that Joren repeated Fenria's words, "The monsters have already passed from this realm…" His hands shook from fear. "Fenria, are the monsters dead?"

"Yes. Their bodies are now under the control of another," she explained.

"Who?" he asked.

"The one who leads the monster's comrades."

"Comrades?" Tearing his eyes away from the rotting bodies of centaurs, trolls, and giant spiders, he found Ossein Guards fighting alongside the beasts. The bodies of the village folk littered the fields. Joren looked at the cart of weapons he'd brought and decided that they weren't going to be of any use against an attack of this magnitude.

"Joren, are you all right?" Barnabas appeared from around the hillside.

"Barnabas… the monsters… the guards…" Joren couldn't form the words that he wanted to say. Instead, he looked to his foster father for guidance.

With grief in his eyes, Barnabas said, "I know." He reached into the cart and pulled on the armor that Joren had crafted.

"You need to retreat. Why are you still fighting?" Joren's rage boiled up in an instant. If it wasn't for the timer on his abilities, flames would have erupted from his hands.

Skills Will Be Available In 5 Minutes

Joren waved away the words that popped up in front of him. "We have no other choice, Joren. Now, go tell your mother that I'll meet her as soon as I can." Barnabas embraced the young man for the second time that day. Joren refused to accept the goodbye he offered.

"I can fight, Barnabas." Joren brought down his hammer to prove his point.

"Your level is not high enough to fight the enemy, Joren."

"You're too young, Joren," Barnabas stated, his tone firm.

"I don't care!" Joren shouted at both his foster father and the artifact.

"The Ossein Master is hunting you, Joren. It would be in your best interest to leave the village before you're captured." Thaddeus's words clicked in Joren's mind when he heard Fenria speak. The thief worked for the Ossein Guild, so it made sense that he was hired by the master to kill Joren and take the artifact. Joren wondered if they had taken over the village's mines for reasons other

than collecting soal stones.

"Will they follow if I run?" Joren asked Fenria.

Barnabas was confused but ignored Joren's strange outburst. "Find your mother. Go now!"

"There's a 98% chance that the enemy will follow if you flee. I will turn off your camouflage until they leave the village."

Joren hadn't known he was under camouflage until then, but he didn't argue. "I left a few soal stones in the forge. You can use them to get by for a while." The young man embraced his foster father quickly before sprinting up the hillside. He looked back when he reached the top, but Barnabas was already distributing the weapons to the village folk. The soal stones lit like beacons in the night while the guardians struck the monsters with their swords and the archers let loose their arrows.

Joren tried to ignore the fact that there were fewer lights each time he glanced back at the battlefield. "Fenria, what are their chances of success?"

Fenria failed to answer, as she had powered down for the remainder of the night.

5

A Troll's Treasure

Joren's legs were sore as he traversed the overgrown trail. The sun was rising, but it didn't bring joy to the blacksmith as it usually did. The light made him feel exposed—a shining target for the Ossein Guild and their undead monsters to set their sights on. However, worrying about his own safety was easier than thinking about the village. He kept repeating to himself, "Barnabas and Marylynn escaped. The children are fast asleep after the long night. The guardians fended off the beasts. Everyone is safe." Joren stared at the dagger that Barnabas had given him before he left. He clutched it tight before tucking it away in his boot.

"Your health levels are dropping, Joren. You need to replenish your energy."

Joren was too tired to be surprised by Fenria's voice. "You don't say," he muttered. "Well, I'm accepting suggestions. I don't have supplies or money, so I'm not sure what you expect me to do." Joren heard an engine humming in the distance.

"According to my system, there is a town five miles north of your location." Fenria's voice was emotionless as usual, but Joren found comfort in her company anyway.

"Is your map up-to-date? You're rather old," Joren asked Fenria. The blacksmith contemplated how he would seem to onlookers, as Fenria couldn't be heard by the people around him. He examined the artifact, taking advantage of the sunlight. There were symbols engraved in the metal. He didn't recognize them, but that didn't mean much coming from an ordinary village blacksmith.

"I was able to scan the land while I was powered down. I needed to confirm that the Inmost Cave still existed within this realm."

Joren didn't comprehend much of what Fenria said, so he decided to ignore it. "Did the Ossein Guild take the bait? Are they following me?"

"Yes, Joren. They left Hopegrove during the night. As promised, I waited to turn your camouflage back on. Your signal is now invisible to them. The guild will have to resort to traditional tracking methods to find you now."

Joren nodded. "You mean like scent and tracks?" He looked back at the trail he'd made in the soil. The forest was full of damp moss and mud, so his boots' prints were obvious.

"The best way to avoid being followed is to unlock your Misdirect Burn ability. You can do this when you reach Level 3."

Joren stopped and rested against a tree, his legs collapsing beneath him. The hammer fell to the ground with a thud, and Joren was glad to be rid of the weight. He reached out and pressed the Menu button. The skills tab explained the strange ability.

Misdirect Burn: Misleads the enemy, so long as a flame continues to burn.

"How long can I keep a fire burning?" Joren asked.

"The length of time increases with your current level. Level 2 only allows you to feed a flame for 15 minutes. It's a good chance to practice your abilities. You must be able to master igniting and smothering your fire at will."

"Will that bump me up to Level 3?" he asked, running a hand through his hair. There were dead leaves tangled in the mess of brunette locks. He shook his head, frustrated.

"Simply igniting your flame won't level you up, but you can use your flames to defeat enemies. It's the easiest route to Level 3 and above," Fenria explained.

Joren exited the menu and sighed. "Where's the nearest enemy?"

"Are you sure that you don't want to rest first, Joren? Your health is gradually declining."

"To hide my tracks, I need to level up, right? Well, I can't rest until I'm hidden from the guild's view. So, let's get this over with." Joren stood with a stiff back and forced himself to pick up the war hammer.

Fenria didn't argue further. She led him to an open field that was 20 minutes to the east. "Where's the enemy?" Joren asked, scanning the empty field.

"It's in front of you, Joren. You should see a rock troll hibernating beneath the shade."

Joren looked closer at the mass that lay next to the forest's edge. What he'd mistaken for a boulder was a living, breathing monster. "Not another troll. I didn't like dealing with the last one very much." The blacksmith cringed, imagining how bad a hit from the solid fists would hurt.

Level 3 Rock Troll

Health 3/3

Joren waited for an ability to offer itself, but nothing popped up in front of him. "How do I activate the abilities without you?"

"Your flames are tied to your emotions and will. Flames are stubborn, which means that you will need to demand rather than ask." Joren wondered if he imagined the smirk in Fenria's voice while he stared at the artifact.

"I need to demand that the flames ignite?" he asked.

"Right now, you need to call the flames. Once I am fully uploaded, then you and the flames will be one and the same." Fenria said such things as if Joren had already agreed to let her take over his body.

"And if I don't want the flames? Can I remove you without dying?" Joren flexed his hands, expecting the fire to appear on its own.

"I don't have access to that information, Joren. The Inmost Cave will have the answers that you seek," Fenria repeated, her voice as soft as a cat's purr.

"Yeah, right." Joren huffed but continued to search for the flames. "I demand that you ignite." When nothing happened, Joren slammed his hammer down on the ground in frustration. When he brought the hammer back up, the weapon was sheathed in fire. Joren laughed, happy to have accomplished something after the long days he'd spent dealing with the guild.

"Approach with caution, Joren. The fire can increase your current emotions. You must learn to control yourself as well as the fire within you," Fenria warned.

"Yeah, yeah. I'll be fine. This is my chance to let off a little steam." Joren chose to ignore Fenria, untrusting of any advice she gave—she was the one slowly taking over his body, after all.

The blacksmith strode toward the troll, allowing the fire from the hammer to crawl up his arm. It burned for a moment, but the pain quickly faded. He stood beside the hibernating troll and watched for any sign of movement. Rock trolls slept for the majority of the year, so it wasn't going to be happy if he woke it up.

"Show me its weak spots," Joren demanded.

A red circle appeared and disappeared a few times along the monster's spine before Fenria said, *"The rock troll's exoskeleton is impenetrable. You must strike it in its soft core."*

Joren rolled his eyes. "So, I have to wake it up?"

"Yes, Joren." She paused before continuing, *"This is a great opportunity to train your skills. An easy win is never a true victory."*

"Well, you're not the one who's hungry and tired, are you? I'd take an easy win any day if it meant I could rest sooner." Joren tapped his foot against the beast's side. It didn't flinch.

"In time, you'll find that there are victories worth fighting for, Joren."

"Enough messing around! How do I wake this thing up?" Joren brought back his hammer and slammed it down on the troll's foot. The vibration from the strike vibrated through the weapon, causing the blacksmith's hands to ache. Still, he brought it down again.

"Retreat to the tree line, Joren," Fenria directed.

Joren begrudgingly did as the artifact told him, waiting under the canopy for the troll to rise from the earth. The monster's spine uncurled, which launched debris across the field. The blacksmith understood why Fenria had told him to fall back. A hit from one of the monster's rock-like scales would have crushed him.

The troll rose, revealing just how grand its height was. Joren felt sweat trickle down his back, worried about the battle to come. He whispered, "What are my chances of success?"

"With your current skills unlocked, you have all the tools

that you need to defeat the rock troll. I will guide you through the process, but the final decisions will be yours, Joren. " Fenria wasn't going to coddle the young man anymore.

"Great," Joren muttered, feeling utterly exposed when the sun peeked through the branches. The monster looked down at its foot and grunted. Suspicious, it scanned the field, and it wasn't long before it spotted Joren stepping out from under the canopy. "Let's get this over with, troll." The blacksmith raised his hammer and pointed it at the monster, daring it to charge.

The creature showed no fear as its long thick legs dashed across the field, the grass caving beneath the intense weight. Joren waited until the troll was upon him before diving to the side. The monster didn't stop when it passed by Joren; instead, it sprinted through the trees. Joren watched in horror as they were flattened by the troll.

"Molten Hammer!" Joren tossed his hammer in the monster's direction, hoping to trap it as he had with the Ossein Guards.

The hammer began to melt, its metal spreading quickly. *"Deactivate Molten Hammer,"* Fenria said.

"What are you doing?" Joren exclaimed, throwing his hands up in frustration.

"The war hammer's level is too low for this ability to succeed. The chances of success are 3% due to the enemy's immense strength."

"Why didn't you say something sooner? Now I don't have a weapon." The blacksmith stared at his cooling hammer.

Reconstruction Will Complete In 20 Minutes

Joren waved the words away. *"All you have to do is ask, Joren. I'm here to guide you on your journey, not lead you to a false victory."*

"Whoever made you must have been a real jerk," Joren commented. He watched as the troll turned around and charged again. He didn't want to ask for help, but fighting without a weapon was daunting. "Show me its weak points."

Red circles appeared, targeting the front of the troll's body. Joren aimed for the closest weak spot on the beast. The troll was moving fast, so Joren led him in another direction. The monster slowed his speed to turn, and that's when the blacksmith activated an ability.

Critical Hit From Burning Roundhouse

2/3 Health Remains

"Well done, Joren." The young man was so pleased with himself that he forgot to move out of the way. With the troll's knee damaged, it was low enough to the ground to reach out and slap Joren aside. Joren's breath was lost, leaving him stunned in the middle of the field.

You've Taken A Critical Hit

Joren groaned but stood up on shaky legs. He charged the monster, intending to take out its other knee. Once he was upon the injured creature, he said, "Activate Burning Ro—"

The troll slapped the blacksmith aside for a second time. Flat on his back, Joren choked, "How am I supposed to reach his core? He's too tall, even down on his knee."

"You have yet to use one of your basic abilities, Joren.

Solar Leap will allow you to reach the height that you need," Fenria explained patiently. The blacksmith wondered if this was amusing to the artifact or if she simply didn't feel anything at all—he didn't know which was worse.

"Thanks," he breathed, unable to expand his lungs fully. The troll was trying to stand, so Joren didn't waste any more time. He ran at the creature and said, "Activate Solar Leap!" The strength he felt in his legs when he jumped was nothing like he'd ever experienced before. The blacksmith peered over the monster's head, watching the trees sway just beyond the battleground. He came down slowly—too slowly. However, he managed to land a hit on the monster anyway.

Critical Hit From Fire Fist

1/3 Health Remains

Joren landed, nearly breaking his ankles in the process. The monster reared back, holding its face with one hand. Fire Fist had obliterated the monster's nose. In anger, the troll grabbed Joren before he could escape and slammed him into the ground, pinning him to the earth.

The blacksmith's limbs were free, but his chest and core were compressed by a giant hand. "Fenr—" The monster added pressure, slowly crushing him beneath its weight. It wanted Joren to suffer.

"You have all the tools that you need to defeat the troll, Joren," Fenria said.

"Are you kidding me!" Joren shouted, irritating the troll further. The monster hovered over the young man, almost mocking him.

Fenria failed to respond, and Joren worried that she'd powered down. Although, he was going to perish if he didn't do something. Despite the pain in his chest, ribs, and hips, Joren thought back to what he'd learned so far. He opened his mouth to activate the ability, but the words didn't come—he couldn't breathe. Then he thought of Barnabas and Marylynn. He thought of his village and all the people who'd helped raise him. It wouldn't have been fair to his family if he wasted all of their hard work.

Flames erupted from Joren's palms. The timer began.

Joren released his fists into the troll's underbelly. The rapid succession stunned the monster, which caused it to loosen its hold on the blacksmith. He could see the monster's health draining. However, Joren's time was nearly gone. He yelled, forcing his arms to pump faster.

Rapid Fire Successful

0/3 Health Remains

Your Abilities Are Locked For 10 Minutes

Joren didn't stop punching the crumbling troll. He ignored the alerts that popped up, allowing his rage to burn.

"Joren, you have defeated the troll. Stand down."

It took a moment for Joren to recognize Fenria's voice. He drew back his bleeding fists.

You Leveled Up!

Misdirect Burn Unlocked

"Well done, Joren. Once your abilities have returned, you can activate Misdirect Burn. It will create various fire trails opposite your current course, so long as your flame is lit. These trails will divert any who follow," Fenria explained.

Breathing was difficult for Joren, but he couldn't help but smile when he saw a small brown pouch lying on the ground. Trolls were known for stealing things from humans. Appreciating the heft of the pouch, he said, "At least I'll eat well when I get to town."

Gold Coins Have Been Added to Items

By the time he entered the town of Steamdale, he'd done more than unlock his Misdirect Burn ability: He'd reached Level 7. Defeating the monsters that constantly harassed humans gave him a sense of pride. However, he was exhausted and starving. Joren spotted a pub and stepped inside, only to be greeted by sour expressions. He sighed. "Are they a threat, Fenria?" he whispered.

"There is a 50% chance that they will attack," Fenria assured.

"Very helpful," he said, the words coated in sarcasm.

"You're welcome, Joren. I will scan the surroundings while you replenish your energy."

Joren didn't argue. He sat down at one of the dirty tables and ordered four bowls of stew and a pitcher of water. The gold coins he flashed at the waitress turned her frown into a smile.

While he waited, he peered at the group forming by the bar. "Surely, you don't think I'm capable of doing such a thing?" a woman's voice questioned. Joren could only catch glimpses of the woman's blonde hair between the men that surrounded her.

"We know that you cheated. Hand over the money or this isn't going to end well for you." More than one of the men mumbled their agreements. Naturally, the largest of the group hovered over the woman.

"Here's your order, sweetheart." Joren ignored the waitress and continued to watch the interaction at the bar. He concentrated on their titles, discerning the chances of the woman's survival.

Level 1 Barfly

Level 6 Thief

Level 30 Nomad

The nomad was the biggest threat. However, Joren couldn't see the woman's title. She was quite a bit shorter than them, which worried Joren.

"I said that I didn't cheat! Why would I risk angering you, fellas? I know that I wouldn't stand a chance against you." The woman's tone didn't match her words, coming off as indifferent.

The nomad slammed a bar stool on the ground, breaking its legs.

Joren stood up, intending to intervene. *"Joren, your health is low,"* Fenria warned.

The woman screamed.

"I don't care," Joren said before flames burst from his palms.

6

A Rogue's Payment

The men didn't notice Joren's flames. Their attention was focused on the woman's laughter. The scream he'd heard had been one of humor, not fear. The nomad stepped back, allowing Joren to read the title that hovered above her head.

Level 20 Rogue

She was covered in leather from head to toe. Joren could see the barest impressions of knives and shurikens under her tight-fitted armor. She was clearly not helpless, but Joren approached anyway. He smothered the flames before saying, "Are these guys bothering you?" The three men turned to Joren, unimpressed.

The woman turned to Joren and smiled brightly. "Get lost, bum. We don't have any treats for you." The men chuckled. Joren frowned, aware of how he looked in his filthy garb. The blonde stepped out of the tight circle and continued to mock the stranger. "Do you know what a bath is?" She waved her hand up and down, scrutinizing Joren.

The blacksmith immediately regretted abandoning his meal. "I see that you have everything under control, blondie. Allow me to remove my filthy self from your presence." Joren bowed sarcastically and turned to leave.

"Awe, did I hurt your feelings? Don't leave so soon." Joren glanced back at the woman, irritated. However, he noticed that the men weren't focused on her anymore; instead, they were watching him.

The blacksmith sighed. "It sounds like bums are your type, blondie. If you want me to stay that badly, why don't you join me at my table? Dinner's on me." Joren smirked when the woman's face twisted into a glare.

The thief was the first one to catch onto the act. "Lyra isn't going anywhere. She owes us some money." He placed his hand on her shoulder, pulling her back. "If she doesn't want to give up the money, then she's going to have to pay in other ways," the thief whispered loudly into her ear.

Joren's flames ignited, but he kept the heat contained under his cloak. The barfly joined the thief, wrapping his arm around the woman's waist. The blacksmith was about to strike when Blondie grabbed the barfly's hand and twisted it unnaturally backward. He screamed, and Joren's flames died from shock.

The thief was next—she grabbed the large hand that gripped her shoulder and hauled the man up and over, sliding her leg back and leaning forward slightly for leverage. He landed with a thud on the pub's floor.

"You bitch," the nomad spat. He was much larger than her, so Joren assumed that he'd have to step in. However, she revealed one of her hidden daggers and stabbed the nomad in the leg.

"What the—" Joren began.

"No time, bum. Let's move," she said, grabbing his arm before darting out of the pub. Joren looked back at his table where the stew had gone cold.

Blondie led him down several alleyways before coming to a stop in front of an abandoned shed. Their breathing was labored, but that didn't stop the rogue from bursting with laughter. "Thanks for the distraction, bum. I owe you one."

Exhausted, the blacksmith said, "My name is Joren."

She met his gaze. "Lyra."

"Nice to meet you, Lyra," he said, unsure if he spoke the truth.

She chuckled, picking up on Joren's negative tone. "See

you around, Joren." She turned to the shed, opened the door, and slammed it shut.

Confused, the blacksmith knocked on the door.

She cracked it open as if she didn't know who it was. "Yes?"

Joren's vision was blurry from hunger. "I didn't get a chance to eat my meal at the pub."

Lyra rolled her eyes. "And?"

Joren leaned against the doorframe, too tired to hold himself up any longer. "Do you have anything to eat? You owe me, after all."

Lyra was suspicious, considering her options.

"Seriously?" he said. The dull ache that had been a constant in his forehead spread to the rest of his skull.

Lyra looked Joren up and down, deeming him not a threat. She opened the door wide. "Fine. Come in."

Joren leaned forward to perform a mock bow once more. That was the last thing he remembered before waking up on a cold cot in the dark.

"Where am I?" he said.

"How have you made it this far in life, bum? Passing out in front of a stranger? You're lucky that I'm not some psycho," Lyra said from the corner of the shed, which wasn't more than a few feet away.

Joren coughed, his stomach retching from pain. "Yes, I'm so lucky," he snapped. It wasn't long before he caught a whiff of spices.

Lyra nodded toward the floor beside Joren. "Eat up."

Joren sat up and grabbed the bowl of soup from the damp ground. He inspected it closely, despite his hunger. There didn't seem to be anything wrong with it. He took a chilling bite and cringed.

"I don't exactly have access to a full kitchen in this little shithole. Don't complain," she said, fidgeting where she sat on a small stool.

Joren swallowed his expression and said, "I can fix it." Before Lyra could ask what he meant, the blacksmith ignited a fire within his palm. He held it beneath the metal bowl until the soup began to boil. The aroma filled the small space, causing Lyra's stomach to growl. Joren ate half of the bowl before forcing himself to stop and give the rogue the rest of the meal, suspecting that it was the only food she had.

The rogue didn't hesitate to scarf down the hot food. In between bites, she asked, "So, what's that thing on your arm? It looks old."

Joren started, debating what information he should share. "Yeah, it is."

She considered him a moment before responding, "That's fine. You don't have to tell me. I was just curious, is all. I recognized the symbols from a cave I sheltered in a while back." Lyra tossed the empty bowl aside and relaxed against the filthy wall.

Attempting to contain his own curiosity, he asked, "Where was the cave at?"

The rogue chuckled. "Wouldn't you like to know, bum?" she taunted.

Irritated, Joren said, "Nevermind." He didn't need the information. Fenria was leading him to the Inmost Cave anyway.

"You should convince the rogue to cooperate, Joren."

Fenria's voice startled the blacksmith, causing his leg to twitch. "Why?" he asked under his breath. The rogue looked at Joren as if she was considering his state of mind. He often did the same.

"My scan was incomplete. I couldn't pinpoint the exact location of the Inmost Cave. You'll have to explore 20 miles of mountainous terrain in order to find it," Fenria explained.

"Why are you just now telling me this?" he spat, forgetting to control his volume.

"I didn't want to burden you until you'd replenished your energy levels, Joren."

"And what if the village is attacked again while I rest? Did you consider that in your calculations? What if they all die because I'm too slow?" Joren planned to remove the artifact when he found the cave and offer it to the Ossein Guild. It wasn't the best option, but if it meant that his village could be spared, then he would do it.

"Well, I've seen enough. I fed you, so I don't owe you anything." Lyra opened the door and motioned for Joren to leave.

"Wait! I'm sorry that I bothered you, but could you please tell me where the cave is? It's important." Joren held his hands up in surrender.

Her laugh was humorless, as she said, "Why would I help some crazy bum?"

Joren could see that Lyra was a hard woman to please. Sighing, he pulled out his stash. "What if I paid you?" He revealed sparkling gold and soal stones.

The rogue slammed the door shut. "Where did you get that?"

"Well, I didn't steal it if that's what you mean." He thought of the monsters he'd collected the money from and deemed those special circumstances. Lyra picked up a soal stone and bit it. "Hey!" Joren swiped the stone from her hand. "Lead me to the cave, and you can have one soal stone."

She reached for the door.

"Two stones."

Lyra grabbed the handle and twisted.

"You can have all the gold and two stones. That's my final offer," he said.

Joren was worried when the rogue didn't release the handle, but she turned and met his gaze. "Deal. We'll leave tonight."

"Why?" he wondered.

"If you haven't guessed already, I've made a few enemies.

It'll be easier to travel in the dark," she explained. She pulled out a couple of small blankets from underneath the cot and handed one to Joren. "Get some rest." Lyra fell onto the cot, leaving Joren to sleep on the rotting wood floor. Still, he smiled.

Joren's sleep was deep, which trapped him in nightmares that played one after another. His family's fearful expressions were the last images he saw before waking to the darkness.

The blacksmith naturally ignited the flames, allowing his hand to act as a lamp in the small shed. "Lyra?" Not finding the rogue, he looked to the door. There, he found a bucket of cold water and a note written in the floor's dirt: *Bathtime.*

Joren dunked his head into the water, allowing the filth from the road to fill the bucket. His hands were next, as well as a rough wash of everything else that he could reach. When he placed the satchel back over his shoulders, he noticed that it was lighter than before. He felt the pockets for his items.

"The rogue relieved you of the gold and soal stones, Joren." Fenria's voice was even, unaffected by the betrayal.

"Why didn't you wake me up?" Joren spat at the artifact. He checked his boot and discovered that she'd stolen Barnabas's dagger, too.

"You were lost deep within your mind, Joren. There was nothing I could have done," she explained.

"What use are you if you can't provide information or protection? I can't wait to get rid of you." Joren's words were born of anger and pain. He couldn't imagine that the insult would hurt a piece of technology, yet Fenria's voice was small when she answered.

"The rogue went north."

"Then that's where we're headed." Joren opened the door, knocking the full bucket aside. The dirty water washed over the rotting floorboards, allowing the blacksmith a moment of petty satisfaction.

The town wasn't as quiet as he expected. Pubs, eateries, and the occasional business lit up the dark street with their soal-powered lights. It was a healthy town, full of thriving people. Jealousy formed in the pit of Joren's stomach. Worry for Hopegrove followed quickly afterward. Those feelings led him to a homeowner's backyard. Clothing flitted in the breeze. Armor had been abandoned on the porch, the owner too tired to continue oiling the leather.

Joren let his clothes fall under the cover of shadows and pulled on the fresh garments from the drying line.

"There's no need to steal, Joren. You can gather more gold from battling monsters," Fenria offered.

"What's the difference between stealing from monsters and these people? I'm having a hard time telling them apart." Joren fitted the armor to his chest, arms, and legs. A fresh cloak completed the ensemble. The only piece left of the village was his boots.

The stench of sweat and blood no longer plagued Joren's nose as he walked down the street. Toward the edge of town, he came across a pawn shop. He stepped inside to find a blonde woman speaking with the owner. Joren's soal stones were laid out on the counter. "I can give you three full pouches of gold for these," the owner said.

"Don't lowball me. This is quality soal. You can tell by the coloring that these came from an Ossein Guild mine," Lyra argued.

Joren slinked behind one of the shelves. The owner considered for a moment. "Fine. I can give you four pouches, but that's really all I can afford."

Lyra shook the man's hand and tucked the gold into a satchel that she didn't have before. She exited the business, and the blacksmith followed. Once they were out of sight, he grabbed her arm. She tried to throw him, but his free palm filled with flames. He hovered the heat near her face. "You took some of my things," he said calmly.

She laughed, but her brows pinched with worry. "I thought that would get you off of your ass." She slowly reached into her bag. "Here." She placed soal stones into his burning hand, minus two.

The flames were smothered. "How?" he asked.

The arm that Joren gripped became fuzzy until she revealed that he wasn't holding onto her forearm, but her cloak. His foster father's dagger appeared with her real arm, the blade pressed against his gut. "Pretty decent illusion, right? Your soal stones are high quality. The owner didn't suspect a thing."

Joren released Lyra and stepped back. "You sold him imaginary stones?" he asked.

"Well, no. After the magic wears off, he'll have high-quality river rocks in his inventory." The woman chuckled and handed Joren his dagger. "Nice piece. Where'd you find it?"

Dumbstruck, he responded, "I made it."

"Of course you did." She smiled and continued, "Ready to go find your mysterious cave?"

Accept Quest Invite From Rogue?

For the first time in a while, Joren's breath came easy. "Yes."

7

A Paladin's Key

"Your conscience must hound you every moment of the day. How do you live with yourself?" Lyra said, teasing Joren as they traversed the uneven terrain.

The blacksmith ran his fingers along his new cloak, appreciating the artistry. "It was the right thing to do. I know what it's like to be without."

Lyra considered Joren before answering, "Still, you had to leave *five* gold coins?"

"What does it matter to you? I said that I would make you a weapon in exchange." The blacksmith's guilt had risen up quickly after stealing the armor from an innocent Steamdale resident.

"Hmmm…what should I have you forge for me? A sword big enough to decapitate a giant? What about a poison dart small enough that it can't be seen by the human eye?" Lyra enjoyed torturing the blacksmith that she'd found in the pub. Although he glared at her often, she refused to fall for his prickly demeanor.

Changing the subject—not for the first time—Joren scanned the jagged mountain edge they currently stood on. "Do you even remember where the cave is, or are we going in circles?" The unfamiliar landscape looked the same to Joren, the gray rocks blending together.

"Yes, village boy. We're almost there." Lyra pointed up at a dip in the mountain's side.

"The signal is strong, Joren. I believe the rogue is correct," Fenria said. Her voice startled Joren after the long night of inner silence. He tripped over his feet, nearly hitting his head on the mountain.

"Shit, thanks," Joren mumbled.

"Don't blame me for your clumsy feet, bum." Lyra stopped below the overhang and bent a knee. "Now, I'll give you a boost up." She held her hands together, expecting Joren to use her for leverage.

"What about you?"

"I can do it much faster alone, trust me." Lyra smiled brightly.

Joren smiled back and ignited his flames.

Solar Leap Activated

The blacksmith had practiced a lot with his ability on the way to Steamdale, so he was confident when he jumped into the air, startling the rogue. "Show-off!" she said from below.

Joren turned, laughing at Lyra's surprised face. The emotion faded away when he turned. "The Inmost Cave…"

Quest For the Inmost Cave Achieved

Accept Paladin's Task?

Joren was about to ask Fenria what the notification meant when a voice fell from above. "Stop there, trespasser. No one may enter holy ground." Joren only had enough time to look up and dive to the side before a figure landed in front of him.

Movement distracted Joren. Lyra flipped upward, landing on her feet where the edge began. "That's how it's done, bum. You can't use fire for everything." She continued to berate Joren until the stranger cleared his throat. She finally looked at the person who blocked their path. "You're still here?"

Joren scrutinized their visitor, wondering what task he would ask them to complete.

Level 32 Paladin

The level may have intimidated Joren if it wasn't for the smallish boy who was underneath the layers of gaudy armor. "Yes. I am the one my sector chose to guard the holy relic. I will be here until the Undying Flame makes an appearance." The paladin's voice was lower than expected, and Joren suspected that he was altering it on purpose.

"You've met?" Joren asked.

Lyra's attitude changed in an instant. "Yes. He let me rest here a few months ago. Isn't that kind, Joren? The paladin told me the best stories while I slept by the fire." Her voice turned sickly sweet, and her smile was insincere. Joren could see right through the act, but the paladin didn't stand a chance.

Rubbing the back of his head nervously, he said, "Call me Anwar."

Lyra continued, "Well, Anwar, we're wondering if you could give us a tour of this lovely cave. Joren is very interested in its symbols."

Anwar turned to Joren and glared. "No one but the Undying Flame can enter here. I cannot make another exception, Lyra." The paladin gripped the hilt of his longsword.

Before Lyra could argue, Joren said, "I accept your task."

"How did you kn—" the paladin began.

Joren revealed the artifact, allowing the rising sun to expose the symbols.

The paladin looked Joren up and down. "Who are you?"

"I'm an ordinary blacksmith from Hopegrove. For whatever reason, this artifact attached itself to me, and I want to remove it." Joren avoided Lyra's gaze, knowing that she was brimming with questions.

Although the paladin was suspicious, he said, "Follow me." The blacksmith and rogue entered the Inmost Cave, listening to the paladin tell the history of the Undying Flame as if he'd shared it many times before.

"In a time long past, the realm was in utter turmoil. The royals were at odds, each family member striving to kill the other. However, while they bickered in their castles, the people suffered. Drought and famine spread across the lands. No one was safe from the guilds who plundered the remaining crops and treasures. That is, until the Holy Paladins decided that the royals were no longer worthy of their loyalty.

"Although, the royals held their position for centuries. They had immense magical power. No one, not even the paladins, could challenge them. That's when an unknown human decided to hunt the legendary phoenix. The creature's magic could not be compared to anything that existed in Aelloria. With its undying soul, the people had a chance to topple the corrupt hierarchy. The human traveled to the highest mountain in the land, knowing that's where the mighty bird had made its nest.

"Being the last of its kind, there were no eggs to steal. So, the human approached the phoenix with force, but nothing could smother its flames." The paladin stopped to admire a depiction of the very scene he described. The cave wall was covered with the legend of the phoenix, its size triple that of any monster Joren had seen.

"The human quickly grew weak, and the mercy of the phoenix was the only thing that allowed the human to survive. So, one day, he asked the creature, 'What must I do to earn your loyalty? The land wanes with corruption and sorrow. Is there nothing I can offer you in exchange for your magic?'

"The phoenix told the human, 'I care not for riches or feasts. My lives have been long and beautiful; however, I lack one crucial experience.'

"'What do you wish for, mighty phoenix? For I will give it to you if it's within my power,' the human begged the creature.

"The phoenix's answer surprised the human. 'I wish for a family. I am tired of existing alone. Give me that, human, and you can wield my power.'

"The human didn't know how to make more of the bird's

kind, nor did he want to sacrifice his own family to the creature. So he offered an alternative. 'I can offer you something better than a family, great phoenix. I can offer you a lifelong companion. Join your soul with mine, and you will never be alone again.'

"The phoenix was displeased. 'What is one human life compared to the thousands that I live? Can you promise me that there will be a human like you who will accept my soul every life cycle?' The human agreed, promising to create a device that would keep the phoenix's wish in every reincarnation."

The paladin led Joren and Lyra to an altar in the center of the cavern, the only light being the torches lining the walls. "Did the human and phoenix defeat the royals?" Lyra asked.

The paladin turned and answered, "Yes. However, evil never fails to reappear. Every reincarnation, the phoenix joins its soul with a human. This brings peace to the realm, and in exchange, the phoenix receives a companion."

"What if the human rejects the phoenix?" Joren asked, his eyes down. The skin itched around the artifact. He set down his war hammer, tired of the weight.

The paladin considered his words before speaking. "The

artifact was created to contain the Undying Flame—the soul of the phoenix. If the human rejected the bond, then it would die without a body to share."

Lyra whispered, "What about the human?"

"The process would have already begun by the time the human decided one way or the other. Meaning, the human would die from the removal." The paladin stepped toward Joren. "Although, any human who rejected the phoenix's prophecy would be an idiot, dooming the realm along with themself."

Joren argued, "It's been a long time since then, right? Surely we have technology and magic far greater than our ancestors did. The realm could survive without the damn bird."

Anwar grabbed Joren's collar, surprising the blacksmith with his strength. "The artifact is a one-of-a-kind item. Immense sacrifices were made during its creation. It's not some flimsy soal stone that runs out of power after a few uses. The Flame is *Undying*. If you're the one it chose, then you're going to accept its offer. There are hundreds of people who would die on the spot to receive an honor such as that!" The paladin released Joren, pushing him back. "Still, I doubt you're the one. Someone like you would never understand the responsibility that comes with it."

Lyra stepped between the paladin and the blacksmith. "How can we test it?"

The paladin revealed a key tucked underneath his shirt. It dangled like a necklace, its gold finish polished to perfection. "Every reincarnation, the chosen human visits this cave. They're to complete the upload by adding their blood to the system." He placed the key into a hidden crevice on the pedestal. "It's a safety measure, so the paladins can keep track of the life cycles."

Joren took Lyra aside. "I need you to do something for me."

Confused, she asked, "What?"

"Take the rest of my soal stones." He placed the stones in her hands. "When I remove the artifact, take it to the Ossein Guild. Trade it for Hopegrove's safety. I know you have no reason to do this for me, but I can't do it myself…" He covered her hands with his, the stones disappearing beneath their grip.

"Joren," Lyra paused, "I can't do that."

"Find Marylynn in the village. She'll give you more money—"

"She isn't leaving with the artifact even if you do reject

the phoenix's offer, blacksmith," Anwar interrupted. "It belongs to the paladins."

"Then why did I find it buried in a soal mine?" Joren snapped. "You didn't even know where it was until now!" His voice echoed in the cavern. "I'm just some random guy. There's no guarantee that I would be able to protect the realm, so I'm going to protect what I can, even if that means I die."

"Joren, our partnership is not meant to be a burden. I awakened upon sensing a kindred spirit," Fenria said.

"You lied to me! This was all a ploy to get me here, wasn't it?" Joren shouted at the void.

"I did not lie, Joren. The artifact that your kind created kept me from accessing the prophecy until we found the cave. Now that we have, I will not force you to join me. If you prefer to die alone, then I will respect your wishes." Fenria's voice was quiet, hurt even. Joren had mistaken Fenria for a piece of technology when she was really the trapped soul of an extinct monster.

"I don't want that! But I will if it means that Hopegrove is safe—that my family is safe." Joren spun around, searching for someone to speak to, but the voice he heard was only in his head. The paladin and rogue looked on, wondering what they could do to help.

"Hopegrove is gone, kid. You left your family to die when you ran," a familiar voice sounded from the cave's tunnel.

"Thaddeus?" Joren whirled, knowing that all three of them were trapped.

The man he'd known before was no more. His core had been replaced with metal, and a soal stone glowed from the center of his chest. "Shocking, isn't it? But hey, that's what I get for underestimating you."

"How did you find me?"

"Those flame trails were a lame attempt, kid. Hiding isn't your strong suit, that's for sure. Well, let's not waste any more time. I'm tired." Thaddeus motioned for the Ossein Guards behind him to advance. The thief retreated, not willing to risk further injury.

"Stop! You are not to set foot on holy ground," the paladin demanded. He unsheathed his sword, its gold soal stone lighting the cavern with warmth.

"Get lost, boy. Our business is with the blacksmith," an Ossein Guard said, uninterested in the paladin.

"The blacksmith is under the protection of the Holy

Paladins. This is your last chance to surrender," Anwar warned. The guards laughed and advanced on Joren. "So be it." The paladin raised his sword, releasing a blinding light, burning the eyes of whoever stared directly at the weapon. "I bathe thee in holy light. Lettest thou be cleansed of darkness and corruption." A few guards stumbled around blindly, holding their burned faces.

"Fenria, was Thaddeus telling the truth? Is Hopegrove gone?" Joren asked while making his way toward the altar. His hammer dragged along the ground, scratching the symbols that were etched into the rock.

"The thief's heartbeat was steady. Hopegrove is lost, Joren," Fenria responded.

Joren stepped up to the pedestal, recognizing the shape of a handprint within the rock. "Then I have nothing left to lose, do I?"

Do You Wish to Complete the Phoenix's Upload?

"Yes," Joren whispered, listening to the sound of blades clanging behind him. Lyra was fighting, too. The whistle of her daggers sounded in the small space.

Joren placed his hand into the imprint, waiting for his blood to be drawn. The pain was intense, but quick, while his hand was stabbed by several tiny shards of rock. He removed his palm and watched his blood absorb into the mountain.

"Joren!" the rogue shouted. The blacksmith whirled, blocking a guard's attack with his hammer. He ignited the flames in his hands and let them crawl up the hammer until the enemy could no longer stand the heat. The guard stepped back, using the length of his sword to keep the flames at bay.

Scanning the cave, Joren saw that there were only three opponents still fighting. The rest of the guards had been blinded or met a quick end with Lyra's blades.

Paladin's Task Accomplished

Upload Complete

Joren roared in anger, advancing on the guard who attacked him. The flames were hotter than before. He could feel them deep in his chest. Joren slammed the hammer down on the guard's sword, trapping the metal beneath the weight of his weapon. He released it, using his Fire Fist ability against the enemy. Once the guard was backed into a corner, Fenria said, *"Activate Burning Roundhouse."*

Although her voice infuriated Joren, he followed her advice and knocked the guard against the mountain with his powerful kick.

Level 16 Guard

0/4 Health Remains

He turned to help the rogue and paladin, but they had taken care of the rest of the enemies. Breathing hard, Lyra asked, "Did anyone else hear that voice?"

The paladin responded, "That was the phoenix." He bowed to the void. "It's a great honor to be in your presence."

"Now that I have full access to the paladin's system, I can communicate with my human's comrades," Fenria explained to everyone.

"I am not your human. This is a business relationship. Nothing more," Joren spat.

"What do you expect of me, Joren?"

"I expect you to help me bring down the Ossein Guild."

8

A Mage's Request

"The Ossein Guild is the strongest one in the realm," Anwar said, sheathing his longsword.

"You can't stop me," Joren warned. Hopegrove was lost. His foster parents could have escaped, but demolishing their home proved that the guild could not be reasoned with.

The paladin chuckled. "Stop the phoenix from bringing down a corrupt organization that's nearly taken over all of Aelloria? I wouldn't dream of it. In fact, I'll join you."

Lyra interrupted, "I thought you couldn't leave the cave?"

Anwar motioned to Joren. "The phoenix has been reborn. I'm free to do as I please now." Joren sent a glare in the paladin's direction. Anwar added, "Even if the phoenix chose some nobody who doesn't deserve the gift he's been given."

"You are worthy," Fenria said to Joren.

"I don't care," Joren responded, realizing that the others

hadn't heard Fenria.

Anwar responded, "It doesn't matter if you don't care, blacksmith. You're going to need help against Malazar. He's the most powerful warlock in the land, specializing in necromancy."

Joren recalled the undead monsters that had attacked Hopegrove. "Malazar is the guild's master," he said. Anwar nodded, the color draining from his young face. Even the gold seemed to leech from his locks. "He took someone from you?" Joren realized.

Swallowing before he answered, the paladin said, "My mentor, two years ago. Malazar was passing through the Holy Paladin's Castle. No one but paladins and apprentices are allowed, but no one can challenge the necromancer." The young man gripped his sword hilt tight. "But my mentor tried—he died a hero."

"Sounds like we have something in common after all, paladin," Joren acknowledged.

"It's sweet that you bonded and all, but—" Lyra started.

The paladin and warrior both exclaimed, "We didn't bond!"

"Whatever," she dismissed, "You're just two people,

phoenix or not. Do you know anything about the Ossein Fortress? What about Malazar's weaknesses?"

The two young men looked at one another, recognizing the large task ahead of them. The paladin spoke first, "I have a source in the city. They're acquainted with Malazar's associates, both current and runaways."

Accept Quest Invite From Paladin?

"That sounds like a good place to start," Joren agreed, turning to Lyra. "Where will you go?"

"Are you kidding? You owe me a weapon. I'm not leaving your side until I have it." Lyra flipped her blonde hair and strode down the cave's tunnel, stepping over fallen guards as she did.

Joren and Anwar stared after her a moment too long before they realized neither of them had moved. *"The rogue has decided to join your party, Joren."* Fenria's voice reminded him of his loss, and the anger returned with vengeance.

"Don't talk to me unless absolutely necessary. I didn't accept you because I wanted to," Joren spat.

Anwar answered, misunderstanding Joren. "Hey, show some respect. I'm a Holy Paladin."

Joren rolled his eyes and said, "You're awfully small for a paladin."

Neither Anwar nor Fenria spoke to Joren until they'd cleared the mountains. It was Lyra who chattered in Joren's ear nonstop, no matter how much he insulted her. It was when the party reached the main road to the city that Joren had finally had enough.

"I'm going to train. You took all of my money, Lyra, so I need to earn some back." Joren stepped off of the road. "Show me the nearest monster, Fenria."

"The nearest monster can be found 50 paces to the west. An adolescent dragon feasts within the berry fields." Fenria's voice was emotionless, and the blacksmith was grateful for it.

"Perfect!" Anwar shouted in Joren's ear.

Startled, Joren said, "What do you want now?"

"The phoenix has sent us on a hunt! I can't wait to bring down the mighty beast. Even a young dragon is difficult to kill," he stated, jogging west with Lyra.

"Hey! No, this was my hunt," Joren sputtered. "Fenria, why did you include them?"

"You need to work as a team to defeat Malazar. I suggest that you start practicing, Joren."

"I didn't know that a phoenix could be spiteful," he said, chasing after his comrades. Fenria said nothing more, but he could feel a tickle of emotion deep in his chest that wasn't his.

***

It wasn't until a blanket of stars hovered overhead that the party tore into the dragon's hide. "A mighty victory for the paladins!" Anwar shouted into the night, the meat's juices dripping down his chin. Lyra chuckled, nibbling on the dragon's tail.

"I'm a blacksmith, and even I know how to keep the food from falling out of my mouth." Joren sent a smirk in the paladin's direction.

The paladin quickly wiped his mouth, peering at Lyra. "Guarding sacred ground doesn't exactly give me the chance to practice my table manners, *chosen one*."

Joren grunted, but Lyra defended the young man. "I bet it gets lonely up there."

"It's not so bad when you know that it's for a cause bigger than yourself," he stated proudly. Though, Joren could see a familiar sadness in the paladin's eyes.

"Your eyes are so blue, Anwar. Natural or a spell?" Lyra asked, fully focused on the paladin.

Anwar blushed and Joren rolled his eyes, digging further into his meal. "Natural. Unlike *someone*."

Lyra and Anwar stared at Joren's eyes, making him fidget. "They're natural, moron. I can't afford a spell as vain as that one."

"They're amber," Lyra observed. "Like a rising flame." Joren met Lyra's kind gaze, unable to break away until Anwar cleared his throat.

"Let's get some rest. Anwar, you're on the first watch. Wake me up when it's over," Joren ordered. He nearly fell into the grass, eager to get away from prying eyes.

"Who says I hav—" the paladin started.

"Joren's health level is the lowest," Fenria stated calmly to everyone. Anwar huffed but agreed. *"Goodnight, Joren."* Joren was beginning to decipher when Fenria kept their conversations private versus public. Her last words were just for him, and somehow, that comforted him as he drifted to sleep.

The days that followed were full of monster hunting and sparring. Joren had reached Level 25 by the time they spotted the city in the distance. He watched as his party's levels climbed with his, though not as rapidly, which he made a point to tell Anwar about constantly. He looked at the paladin now, scrutinizing his perfectly-polished armor.

Level 36 Paladin

"Do you know where your source is? The City of Aelloria is large," Joren questioned. Puffs of smoke rose up from the city, its technology much more advanced than the outer villages. Pipes connected all the buildings together, their steel frames unbreakable. The hum of engines nearly drove Joren to madness, reminding him of the time he spent living on the city's streets as an orphan.

"Part of my job is observing the main crime hubs. I checked in with fellow paladins every day, so I would know where to go if I was ever called to action," he explained.

"Impressive," Lyra commented. Joren glanced at her, but she was already staring at the blacksmith, her eyes twinkling with mischief.

Joren quickly looked away, ignoring the rogue. "So, where

do we go?"

"Mage Kolos can be found at Lore Emporium," Fenria answered. *"I have the coordinates."*

"How did you know?" Joren asked, suspicious.

"Paladin Anwar and I spoke while you slept this morning, Joren."

Startled by the knowledge that she could speak while he was unconscious, Joren didn't say a word. Instead, he nodded and walked faster. "Hey, slow down! We have a lady present," Anwar said.

Lyra snickered and sprinted forward. "Come on!"

The party raced into the city, ignoring the onlookers as they followed Fenria's directions. Soon, they were staring up at a glowing sign that read, *Lore Emporium: A Spell For Every Need.* They stepped inside.

Quest For Mage Kolos Completed

"Does this mage own a magic shop?" Lyra asked, running her fingers down a line of skulls on the shelf.

"I can't decide if hiding in plain sight is clever or stupid," Joren said, staring at a glass of frozen human eyes.

"Oh, definitely clever." A tall man appeared before them, leaning against the counter as if he'd always been there—maybe he had. His white hair was stark against the shop's black walls.

Joren turned to Lyra and whispered, "I bet you like his eyes more than Anwar's."

Lyra snorted but quickly disguised it with a cough. The three of them were ensnared by the stranger's glowing blue eyes. Clearing his throat, Anwar said, "Mage Kolos, it's an honor to meet you. I am Paladin Anwar and these are my comrades, Lyra and—"

"The Undying Flame," Kolos answered. The mage disappeared and appeared again in a cloud of mist. He grabbed Joren's arm, studying the artifact.

Joren jerked his arm away and raised his hammer toward the mage. "Hands off."

The mage lifted his hands in surrender but the smirk on his face said otherwise. "I know someone who's been searching for that for a very long time."

"Malazar," Joren stated. "We've come to request knowledge. We can pay you."

"Oh, really? What can you offer me other than that old

trinket on your arm?" Kolos teased, though the party couldn't discern if the mage was serious or not.

Lyra offered up her stash of soal stones and gold. "Will this be enough to answer a few questions?" Joren looked at Lyra, shocked. She glanced back at him and shrugged. "I can always steal more."

The mage strode up to Lyra, and both Joren and Anwar tensed. He picked up a soal stone and examined it closely. "These are quality soal stones, but alas, I don't deal in trades such as this." He waved, dismissing the overly-generous offer.

"What do you want then?" Joren asked.

"I want to speak to the phoenix," Kolos answered. His angled features were almost angelic; however, Joren could see secrets lying beneath the sweet smile.

"You have to join our party before you can speak to the great phoenix, and I'm assuming we're not a good enough bunch for someone like you, right?" Anwar said, his lips pinched with the bitter admission.

Level 44 Mage

The mage tapped his finger against his lips, considering. "I'd love to continue this conversation further, but it seems that you were followed." Kolos waved his hand over Joren's arm, and the artifact disappeared.

"Where did Fenria go?" Joren demanded.

"I'm here, Joren. The mage has hidden me from sight." Fenria paused as if she was thinking. *"Malazar is a gifted warlock. He evaded my scans. I'm sorry."*

"The Ossein Guild's master is *here*?" Joren said, a chill crawling up his spine.

The mage nodded. "You don't have the artifact. Are we clear?" The mage's calm demeanor had turned to stone.

Lyra interrupted, "Why aren't we running?" She unsheathed her knives and turned toward the door.

Joren blocked her path with an outstretched arm. "Because he's already here."

9

A Party's Encounter

The bell rang when the shop's door opened. Mist and the stench of decay invaded Lore Emporium. A large, hooded figure passed through the doorway, an undead entourage lingering behind him. Joren immediately recognized Thaddeus amongst them, but he was no longer the same man.

Level 1 Undead Thief

Joren took Lyra's arm and led her behind the counter.

"Hide," he whispered in her ear. He removed a soal stone from her satchel, forcing it into her hands. "Don't come out until he's gone."

"Joren—" she started.

The blacksmith shook his head, refusing to argue.

The rogue recited her illusion spell, disappearing from view. The only evidence was the slight disturbance of dust on the shelves as she walked past them. Anwar caught the interaction, nodding to Joren. The paladin grabbed the hilt of his sword, but Kolos placed a hand over his, stopping him. "Not yet," he mouthed.

The mage stepped in front of the party. "Welcome, Master. I can't believe someone as great as yourself decided to pay my little shop a visit. It's a great honor, truly." The mage bowed slightly, the man's white mane falling over his eyes.

Although the undead stayed outside of the shop, Malazar's presence was enough to incite fear in every single person who stood before him. The hair stood erect on the back of Joren's neck. He couldn't see or feel Fenria on his arm, but he knew that she was there. Her presence was one he was slowly adjusting to. It was as if he'd grown another heart and it beat in tandem with the original. A foreign sensation, but not an unwelcome one.

The mage didn't rise until Malazar had removed his hood. Joren had expected it to be a man beneath, but what he saw was something else entirely. A skull stared back at the mage, its eyes empty and black. His face was bare, without skin to express emotion. However, Joren could feel the darkness that he exuded. If the warlock had ever been a man, the human part of him had been abandoned long ago.

The warlock's black-and-crimson armor shifted as he moved. His onyx staff crawled outward, wrapping around the warlock's arm like a snake. "Kolos, it's been too long since you've visited. Where is the research I requested?" The voice that escaped the skull's mouth was raspy and strangled.

"I apologize, Master. The tomes I required took an extended period of time to find. The report will be finished shortly," the mage said, his head lowered submissively. It was a startling contrast to how the man had acted before.

The warlock focused on the blacksmith, eyeing his bare arm. "Your name," he demanded. Joren paused a moment too long. Malazar turned toward the counter and uttered foreign words. A woman was screaming in the next moment.

"Lyra!" Anwar shouted. Lyra's illusion broke, her skin blackening from the warlock's spell.

"Stop!" Joren demanded. The warlock stared at the rogue, his eye sockets swirling with gray mist.

Anwar unsheathed his sword and lunged at Malazar. The warlock's staff shifted. Joren knew that the paladin was too distracted by Lyra to notice. The blacksmith launched himself forward, knocking Anwar out of the way. Joren met the attack, his lungs locked beneath the warlock's magical hold. Thankfully, Lyra stopped screaming.

"Your name," Malazar breathed into Joren's shocked face. He tried to form the word, but he couldn't stop staring at the warlock's title.

Level 100 Necromancer

Health 10/10

"What did you say, boy?" he asked, a chuckle rumbling in his chest.

"J-Joren," the blacksmith said, breathless from the spell the warlock had trapped him in. Joren considered igniting his flames, his palms opening.

"Do not engage this enemy, Joren. Your chance of success is 0%," Fenria warned.

Joren wanted to argue, so he could fight for his party— fight for his village.

"I know what you want, Joren. Don't give in to your emotions." Her voice was soft and soothing. It convinced the blacksmith to stand down and feign ignorance.

"I'm looking for a Joren. He has something I need." Joren's breath returned, and he fell to the floor. "You see, I have a dream for Aelloria, young man." The warlock abandoned the blacksmith and began pacing around the shop. He visited Lyra where Anwar held her, the rogue's black curse receding.

"Stay away from her," Anwar threatened, his sword at the ready.

The warlock was amused, ignoring the young paladin. He locked eyes with Joren from across the room. "As a young warlock, I was ignorant. I believed that life was precious. But it wasn't until death greeted me that I felt a sense of peace. I was complete for the first time in my existence." He waved to the undead monsters outside. "The cycle is what I strive to master. These creatures are not complete until their souls are in my grasp. Bodies are empty, useless. But souls…" He found his way back to Joren. The mage stayed in the corner, avoiding the warlock's attention.

Joren stood, trying to ignore the warnings that Fenria shouted at him. "Your undead army destroyed my home. It sounds like you've found a use for them," Joren spat. The blacksmith didn't care about the warlock's dreams—he just wanted to end him.

Malazar's face didn't budge, but Joren could sense that he enjoyed his pain. "You mean that little village full of failed miners? Well, I can't disagree that the body has *some* uses." Joren nearly gagged on the scent of death that wafted from his armor. "But don't worry. I made sure to hunt down every single one of those villagers and add them to my forces. They're experiencing bliss, and only when I have the power to recover their souls will they finally be at peace."

The warlock reached out with bony fingers and gripped Joren's arm. "But I can't do that without the Undying Flame." His voice had transformed from calm to furious in an instant. "Where is it?"

Joren was reeling from what Malazar had revealed. He couldn't stop imagining his foster mother and father, their faces rotting on the battlefield. Joren imagined having to fight against his own family—it nearly broke him. Warmth was building in his palms when the mage stepped forward. "It appears that young Joren has sold the artifact to the paladins." He turned to a confused Anwar. "As repayment, they offered him an apprentice to guard him and his lady friend from the Ossein Guild." The mage smirked. "Clearly, the paladins are not as noble as they claim to be."

The mage stepped aside, eyeing Joren. The warlock pushed Joren aside. "And the legends said that the host would die if the phoenix was to be removed." He turned back to Joren, red orbs forming in his eye sockets. "*Clearly*, we can't take every detail for granted."

Malazar went to the door, and the party dared to breathe a sigh of relief. The undead could be seen fighting amongst themselves beyond the stained glass window. The door's hinges creaked when the warlock pulled the handle. "Kill them all," he ordered the undead.

"Master, is it really necessary to—" the mage began, stepping between the party and the doorway.

The mage was thrown backward, colliding with a shelf full of glass containers. Each one released some form of magic upon shattering. Blizzards and swarms of flies circled the shop. There was no time for the party to react before Malazar sent his staff directly through Kolos's core, impaling him as if it was a spear. "I don't tolerate tardiness." The staff was summoned back, settling onto Malazar's arm again. "You're as useless as that thief."

Without another word, he disappeared into a cloud of black, allowing his corpses to enter the shop. The party looked to Kolos, but he was no longer conscious. The spell he had cast on Fenria dissipated, revealing the artifact. "Anwar, get Lyra out of here. I'll burn them with Fenria," Joren said.

"No way!" Anwar abandoned a recovering Lyra just in time to stop Joren from igniting his flames. "We don't know where he has eyes," the paladin whispered.

"The paladin is correct, Joren. I cannot help you defeat this enemy. Until you are ready to face Malazar, you will have to be discreet."

"Damn it!" Joren shouted, shoving his sleeve down. "My order still stands. Take Lyra and go!" The blacksmith raised his war hammer and swung it at the nearest corpse. Its skull caved inward, but the rest of it continued to move forward.

A rotting gnome leaped from the floor. It had nearly

locked its claws on Joren's shoulder when a dagger soared through the air, pinning it to the wall. The paladin and warrior turned to Lyra. "We're not leaving you, so stop fighting us!" The rogue picked up a mysterious bottle and threw it against the doorframe. The party retreated behind the counter, dragging the mage with them. A rainstorm fell down on the undead, slowing them for a moment.

"Is there a door in the back?" Anwar asked.

"Yes, but Malazar has surrounded us. There's nowhere to go," she said, her breathing rapid. She grabbed Joren's hand, and said, "We need the mage's help."

Joren examined the bleeding mage on the ground. "He's not in the best condition right now, Lyra." The storm faded away, allowing the undead to advance without issue. The party used furniture as a barricade around the counter and Lyra continued to throw mysterious spell bottles, but those only slowed one or two corpses at a time.

Watching the paladin and rogue struggle to fend off the horde, Joren made a decision to ignite his flames, regardless of Malazar.

"Rogue Lyra and Paladin Anwar, I wish you luck in this battle. However, Joren will not be a part of it," Fenria announced to the party.

"What are you talking about?" Joren questioned. The blacksmith didn't receive an answer before he collapsed.

System Will Reboot In 1 Hour

***

Lyra and Anwar looked to one another, grateful that Fenria had taken control of Joren. Anwar raised his sword and summoned his light, blinding the corpses that surrounded their barricade. However, these beings didn't feel pain. They kept advancing, despite their blindness.

Lyra searched the shelves for healing potions, desperate for the mage's assistance. Kolos's blood had spread across the floor, the party slipping on it. The rogue grabbed a golden bottle. She tried to pour it into a bowl, but it wasn't liquid. Instead, she smashed the bottle against the ground near the mage's wound.

Lyra was startled by what the bottle shared. Mist and sunshine mixed until they formed the shape of a woman. Her hair was the color of fire, falling down her back in waves. Her skin was fair and as smooth as silk.

"Kolos?" the woman muttered. She turned to Lyra. "What happened?"

Lyra snapped out of her shock and said, "He was stabbed

with Malazar's staff. Can you help him?"

The crimson-haired woman nodded, determined. "Consider this my repayment, mage." The woman's hands glowed with light. The warmth spread to the mage, mending his wound slowly.

Lyra discovered that Anwar had lost his sword to the horde and struggled to keep the barricade upright. His armor was covered in blood, and she suspected that it was not from the undead. The rogue abandoned the mage and went to Joren. He wasn't injured, which lightened the weight in her chest.

The paladin said, "Who the hell is that?" Anwar fell to his knees, but the young man continued to hold the wall.

Before Lyra could answer, Kolos awakened. "Rafaela?" he said, his voice full of pain.

"Get us out of here, Kolos," the mysterious woman demanded.

The mage scanned the area and nodded. He beckoned Lyra over, and said, "I'll take those soal stones now." The mage smiled, but it was forced.

Lyra emptied her stash into his hands and watched as he crushed them in his grip. He stood with the help of Lyra and the stranger. With the powder, the mage drew a circle on the floor and uttered words from ancient times. "Get in," he ordered.

The mage and woman disappeared from sight when they stepped into the portal. Lyra dragged Joren and his hammer into the circle with her. Anwar didn't follow until he was sure that everyone was in. He let the barricade drop behind him, diving into the portal after his party members.

10

A Healer's Hands

Joren opened his eyes to find strands of red hair hovering over his chest. Delicate hands pressed against his heart, but the ache was in his head. He found it difficult to move, so he took his time waking, merely listening to the stranger's voice.

"Kolos found me on the outskirts of the city. A sector had been attacked by Malazar's forces, leaving the residents for dead. I offered them the chance to heal and run." She paused, recalling the incident. "Sadly, I wasn't able to save everyone. One of the deceased awakened as an undead. I didn't see the corpse until it was already upon me." The woman removed her hands from his chest, and the light emanating from them faded away.

"So, Kolos hid you in a bottle?" Lyra asked. Joren sat up suddenly, startling the group.

The stranger smiled at Joren and continued, "My healing abilities stem from light. He placed me in a bottle of sunshine while I recovered. Without him, I would have become one of the warlock's minions."

Lyra knelt down beside Joren and grabbed his hand. "I'm glad you're okay, bum."

Joren rolled his eyes and laid back down.

"My magic is born of light, as well," the paladin added. He sat on an obnoxiously blue chair, his sheath empty.

"What happened to your sword?" Joren asked, his voice rough with sleep.

Anwar pinched his lips, irritated that Joren had noticed so quickly. "I lost it trying to protect *you*, blacksmith."

"I didn't need protection. I could have helped." Joren stood, his knees weak. Lyra helped the blacksmith balance, but he quickly nudged her aside. He ignored her hurt expression and said, "Fenria, what did you do to me?"

Reboot Complete

The ache in Joren's head vanished, leaving anger in its wake. *"We could not risk Malazar discovering our union, Joren. I rebooted our system while your party handled the encounter."*

"That wasn't your call to make." Joren's flames ignited, and everyone but Lyra backed away.

"The phoenix was right to hide you, Joren. If Malazar had

realized you still had the artifact, then he would have come back to finish what he started," the mage's voice carried from across the large room. He laid on a luxurious bed with a bandage wrapped tightly around his chest. He motioned to the stranger. "And this is Rafaela. You should thank her for saving us."

Rafaela blushed. "*You* saved us. I merely tended to your wounds."

The mage smirked but didn't argue. "This is my safe house, so to speak. It's under the city and strongly warded. Malazar will not find us here." He looked at Joren's hands. "So, please don't burn it down."

Joren huffed and smothered his flames with a closed fist.

"This is good. It'll give us a chance to rest and come up with a plan. Kolos had already agreed to share any information that he has with us," Lyra said, her eyes hopeful.

"Plan? That *monster* is at an unimaginable level. He had us under his thumb the whole time, and he barely did anything." Joren struggled to control the raging flames that boiled beneath his skin. "The whole reason I did this was for my village." The blacksmith retreated when Lyra reached out to him. "But they're gone now—nothing but corpses."

"So is my mentor! Malazar has taken a lot of lives, which is why he needs to be stopped," Anwar said, his voice cracking with emotion. He quickly hid his face, standing to challenge Joren. "You accepted Fenria's bond. You can't take that back now!"

"I'm not taking it back! But that doesn't mean that I have to fight, either. I don't care what your legends say, this bird is not the answer to your problems," the blacksmith spat.

Fenria stayed quiet, but the healer interjected. "Kolos explained what you are, Joren. I grew up listening to stories about the mighty phoenix and the hero who joined souls with her. Every reincarnation, they work together to bring peace to the realm." She didn't try to reach out to Joren but she held his gaze. "We need that hero more than ever right now."

Level 36 Healer

The words that the healer spoke were meant to encourage Joren, but all they did was push him further into the abyss that was his broken heart. He picked up the hammer that he'd forged with such care and placed it in the paladin's hands. "There's your hero," he said before retreating from the room.

Joren stepped into what he expected to be a bedroom, but instead, it was a dark space filled with stars. He slammed the steel door shut behind him and sat in the middle of the room, content with his solitude. Fenria didn't try to speak to Joren, and he didn't reach out to her either.

For hours, the blacksmith sat under the stars, admiring the work that the mage had put into the illusion. Eventually, Joren removed Barnabas's dagger from his boot. It was the first weapon that he'd ever forged. He almost smiled at the bend in the blade, knowing that it was far from a perfect creation. Still, his foster father had accepted the gift with a proud smile.

"I'm never going to see them again," Joren told the stars.

However, it wasn't the stars who answered. "This was the first room I spelled when I was done with the build," Kolos said from the open doorway. Joren had failed to recognize the stream of yellow light that fell across the dark room.

"It's nice," Joren said, realizing how stiff he'd become after sitting on the hardwood floor for hours. The mage took a seat next to him. "Your wound is healed," Joren observed.

The mage tapped his chest, only a thin vest covering the upper half of his body. "Rafaela is a talented healer. We're lucky to have her in our party."

"We?" Joren asked.

"Of course. You think I wouldn't join you after all that we've been through together?" The mage winked. "Malazar has been getting under my skin for centuries. I was just waiting for the right time to turn against him."

Joren cringed, unsure how he felt. "Well, I wish all of you the best of luck."

The mage didn't argue, simply watching the stars rotate with the blacksmith. It wasn't until Joren had forgotten about Kolos's presence that he said, "I kept my end of the deal. It's your turn." Joren turned to the mage, perplexed. "I want to speak to the phoenix," he clarified.

"Oh, right. Well, I don't really control her," Joren began.

"Mage Kolos, what would you like to ask me?" Fenria's voice was quiet, but as clear as the stars above.

"Your voice is more beautiful than I imagined," the mage said, his eyes lighting up.

"Fenria doesn't respond to stuff like—"

"Thank you, Kolos. I'm glad to have a use for it after so much time has passed," she answered. Joren closed his mouth, realizing that he'd been treating her like a machine that was incapable of emotion.

The mage smiled at Joren as if he knew what the blacksmith was thinking. "Fenria, since I heard the legend of the great phoenix, I've had one burning question on my mind." The mage inhaled, readying himself for the answer. "Did joining souls with the hero give you the happiness that you longed for?"

Joren was surprised by the question but he didn't speak. They both waited for Fenria to answer, and Joren's heart was pounding by the time she did. "The happiness I longed for was found, but not in the way that I expected."

Joren couldn't contain his curiosity. "In what way then?"

"I expected the companion to bring me joy simply by being by my side. However, my happiness was only ever felt when my partner was happy. If they were sorrowful or furious, I would also be those things." Fenria paused, and the next time she spoke, her tone had altered to one Joren's foster mother had used to console him when he was young and lonely. "My answer, Kolos, is yes. As long as my hero is happy, I am content."

The mage couldn't contain his awe. "It seems that you found a family, after all, Fenria."

There was joy in her voice when Fenria answered, "Indeed."

The mage stood to leave but paused to tell the blacksmith, "You've made friends, Joren, but whether you accept them as family is up to you." The mage left the young man to ponder his words, closing the door behind him.

It wasn't long before Joren left the star-filled room, asking Kolos if there was anywhere that he could hunt. The mage directed him to the city's sewers, which was less than appealing, but the blacksmith couldn't face the party members yet.

Joren spent a few days in the sewers, gaining experience and avoiding unwanted conversations. Fenria only spoke when she needed to guide Joren through a battle with a sludge critter or scaled beast. The blacksmith ate cursed snails for nourishment and boiled his drinking water in his hands.

He walked through the tunnels, trapped in his dark thoughts. Eventually one of those thoughts spilled from his lips. "I'm sorry that you're stuck with me, Fenria. You deserve better."

The phoenix took several moments to answer. *"I've experienced countless life cycles, Joren. In that time, I've befriended many heroes. Each one was unique in personality, strength, and weakness. However, they all shared one recurring trait."*

"Oh, yeah. What's that?" Joren asked, kicking aside a dirt gremlin.

"They suffer before they rise."

Joren didn't speak to Fenria for the remainder of the outing. Only when he was completely drained did he return to the mage's hidden home. Stepping through the doorway, he was greeted by a giant slime beast. It stood in the middle of the living area, its skin dripping with ick.

Lyra appeared with Joren's hammer in her hands. The slime beast set its sights on her and lunged. Joren was a moment away from burning the beast alive when Lyra's form shifted and Anwar stood in her place. He took the hammer and slammed the sharp end into the beast's throat. The creature didn't collapse but rather vanished into thin air.

Joren turned and found that Lyra was at the opposite end of the room, focusing on the monster. She held a soal stone in her palm. "Successful exercise, everyone," the mage said from his seat in the corner. The blacksmith relaxed, realizing that there was never a monster at all.

Rafaela appeared beside Joren and said, "Care to join us?"

Joren hid his surprise and said, "I just came back for a shower."

Anwar wrinkled his nose. "Not a bad idea, blacksmith." He set down Joren's hammer. "How have you been carrying this thing around? It weighs more than a rock troll."

Anwar's attempt at a compliment left a bitter taste in Joren's mouth. The blacksmith left them without saying another word, spending a long time in the bathing area. When he came out, Lyra was waiting for him with a bowl of hot soup. "Hungry?" She used the food as bait, leading him to the familiar stars next door.

"Thanks," he said, digging into the first real meal he'd had in days.

"I'm worried about you," she said, taking his hand after the bowl was emptied.

The blacksmith tried to remove her grip but she held on tight. "Stop pushing us away," she demanded.

"What do you want from me?" Joren asked, allowing her hand to stay.

"I—We want you to fight." She scooted closer to the blacksmith.

"We can't stop Malazar, Lyra. You didn't see what I did." Joren found himself squeezing her hand back. "You'll all die—just like they did."

"Like your family? Do you think they would want you to give up?" Lyra said, her voice loud in the small space.

"I'm just an ordinary blacksmith from a dying village. How am I supposed to help?" Joren argued.

"Do you think you're special, Joren? Well, you're not!" Her body shook with anger, and Joren was smart enough to stay silent while she spoke. "Rafaela is an orphan from the river tribe, Kolos was a slave before someone discovered his magic abilities, and Anwar's parents sold him to the paladins because they didn't want him." Lyra lowered her voice. "*Everyone* here has come from nothing."

"And what 'nothing' did you come from, Lyra?" Joren asked, his gaze meeting hers.

The rogue released his hands and walked to the doorway.

"If you want to know, our party will be training in the other room." Lyra smiled, but it was forced. Joren felt the urge to follow the rogue, but instead, he continued to sit in the darkness.

Three days passed before Joren had the courage to leave the star-filled room. His eyes were sunken with grief and his stomach growled with displeasure. However, he only wanted one thing. The party faced the blacksmith, and Joren said, "Take me to Hopegrove."

11

A Warrior's Phoenix

"That's not a good idea," Anwar stated with the hammer in his hands.

"Malazar thinks we're all dead, right?" Joren argued. "There's little risk."

Anwar shook his head. "Once he realizes that the paladins don't have Fenria, he'll be looking for you."

Lyra interjected, "I think it's a good idea. We can't stay down here forever." She took Joren's hand in front of everyone and the blacksmith didn't pull away. He peeked at Anwar, but the paladin's expression was neutral.

"Agreed. There are people who need my help," Rafaela said. Joren nodded, grateful for the healer's support.

The party turned to Kolos. The man lounged on the sofa, his feet propped up on a giant quartz crystal. "I think you're outvoted, Anwar." The mage smirked. Snapping his fingers, a staff appeared in his hands. "Rafaela, you'll need this where we're going."

The healer took the long, wooden staff from the mage. The top encased a golden orb that shimmered in the light. "My staff… Thank you for rescuing it. I thought I'd never see it again."

The mage stood and said, "Let's get a move on then." He exposed a bag full of soal dust and poured it around the party. "Prepare yourselves," he warned, before uttering the words that sent everyone plummeting through the portal.

Joren didn't let go of Lyra's hand until he saw a familiar house. The party had landed across from his foster parent's home. The door had been torn from its hinges, similar to the rest of the shelters. The surrounding village looked as if it had been abandoned centuries prior. The greenery had grown over the gates and the crops had withered away.

"The fields," Joren whispered.

"Activate Solar Leap," Fenria said. Joren was able to reach the fields where he last saw Barnabas in only a few jumps, but the battle hadn't left any corpses behind. *"Malazar stole the bodies. I'm sorry, Joren."*

"It's not your fault. I knew I wasn't going to find them, but I couldn't stop myself from hoping," he said, emotion crawling up his throat.

"They wouldn't want you to lose hope," she said.

Joren nodded and took his time returning to the group. He wanted to meet Lyra's worried stare, but he kept his head down and walked past them. The blacksmith found himself at his old forge. Stepping inside, he scrutinized the damage. The villagers had scoured it for supplies, and the monsters had torn it to shreds.

"So, this is where you spent your time, blacksmith," Anwar said from the doorway.

Joren didn't turn around when he said, "Many years. The village lost its last blacksmith to the guild when I was 12. So, I picked up the hammer and taught myself to craft."

"When I was 12, my mentor made me battle against a baby dragon. Its flames were just as hot as an adult's."

Anwar righted the crooked table. "You could say that we were both born of fire."

Joren laughed for the first time in days. "You could say that." He rubbed the back of his neck, recalling the long nights he spent bent over the furnace.

Joren's war hammer slammed down beside him. "Paladins don't use hammers. We prefer swords and spears. You know, *useful* weapons."

The blacksmith smiled and said, "Are you sure that you're a paladin? Kolos seems to think that you're an apprentice."

Anwar growled in frustration. "Even *you've* heard him call me that? Can you tell him that I'm a fully-trained paladin? He doesn't seem to believe me," Anwar whined.

"I'll get right on that," Joren said. Before the two party members departed the forge, Joren noticed that his secret compartment was covered. Curious about the soal stones he'd left for his family, he removed the covering. The soal stones were gone, and in their place was a piece of paper.

My son,

I don't know where you've gone, but we cannot stay in the village any longer. You can find us at the place where we found you.

With all my heart,

Marylynn

"They're alive," Joren whispered.

"Who?" Anwar asked, his head peeking around Joren's shoulder.

"My family. I know where they are!" Joren picked up his hammer and sprinted to the others. The party hadn't gone far—merely searching for supplies.

"The villagers are at Fairy's Marsh," Joren announced.

The mage was surprised. "I've been to that place. How did magicless humans manage to get past the cyclops who guards it?" he asked.

"I've done it before. I came and went when the monster left to hunt. My family found me on the outskirts of the marsh, starving to death." Joren couldn't contain the excitement and worry that coursed through his blood.

Quest to Fairy's Marsh

Send Invite to Party Members?

"Will you come with me?" Joren asked, preparing for the rejection.

4 Invites Accepted

The mage drew another portal and the party landed in a forest a few miles from Hopegrove. "Now what?" Lyra asked.

Task: Defeat the Marsh's Guardian

"Oh, no," Joren said before scanning the trees for movement.

"Activate Fire Fist, Joren," Fenria said.

The party didn't have a chance to prepare before a monstrous cyclops stepped through the trees, its fangs longer than Joren's arm. "Did you have to drop us right in front of the guardian, Kolos?" Anwar asked, irritated and weaponless.

Level 50 Cyclops

Health 5/5

The mage summoned a short sword and handed it to Anwar. "Here, you can use this."

"What am I supposed to do with this?" The paladin waved the short blade through the air. "Pick its teeth with it?"

"I just thought it fit your size," the mage said, smirking

while he created a giant orb of water. The party didn't have time to argue further, the cyclops taking Anwar's sword-waving as a challenge.

Joren activated his Solar Leap and landed a hit to the monster's jaw. Once he found earth again, the mage surrounded the creature's head in water, cutting off its air supply.

Critical Hit From Fire Fist

4/5 Health Remains

Solar Leap: 10 Second Cool Down

The monster grew desperate and charged Kolos. The mage stared him down, assuming that the beast would collapse before he could reach him, but the paladin knocked him out of the way. The water orb dissipated when the mage lost his concentration.

"This is how it's done, mage." Anwar jumped onto the monster's foot before it could crush him and stabbed its leg, sending the blade through its shin.

Critical Hit From Paladin's Sword

3/5 Health Remains

The paladin was thrown off quickly, which left him

without a weapon once again. "Was that sword too heavy for you?" the mage mocked from the marsh, where the paladin had pushed him.

"Stop messing around!" Lyra and Rafaela shouted.

Lyra sent her blades flying toward the monster's eyes, and she managed to blind one of them. Rafaela knelt beside a winded Anwar, healing him instantly. She looked to Kolos and said, "Are you going to help or just stand there all day?"

Critical Hit From Rogue's Blade

2/5 Health Remains

"As you wish, my lady," the mage said, summoning a ball of fire.

Joren nodded to the mage, and the blacksmith activated his Solar Leap again. This time, he aimed for the monster's heart, raising his weapon high. The mage sent his ball of fire into the monster's other eye, so it wasn't able to block Joren when the blacksmith landed his hit.

Critical Hit From Mage's Flames

Critical Hit From War Hammer

0/5 Health Remains

Joren landed without grace, rolling through the wet forest soil. Rafaela was quick to find him and offer her healing hands. "Thank you, Rafaela," he said, watching the light fade from her palms. The woman nodded and helped Joren stand.

"Joren!" a woman's voice called from above.

The blacksmith couldn't contain his joy when he looked up and saw Marylynn staring down at him from the floating crystals. "Marylynn, are you okay?" Joren yelled back.

"Who cares? Get up here!" she shouted, her soothing voice traveling on the wind with ease.

"What the hell are those things?" Anwar asked, plucking his sword from the fallen monster's leg.

"The fairies place their dead in the water. The magic absorbed into the marsh's crystals over time until they could fly just as well as the fairies," the mage explained, staring at the floating minerals with admiration.

The party was entranced by the natural occurrence, but Joren didn't care. He took the vine that Marylynn lowered for them, climbing the distance in moments. The blacksmith embraced his foster mother, breathing in her scent of flowers and bread. "I've been so worried, Joren.

What happened to you?" she asked.

Joren let a tear slip down his cheek but wiped it away before the rest of the party could join him. "It's a long story. Where's Barnabas?" he asked, peering behind her. The crystals were hollowed out by humans long ago, so the space was large. It held several dozen people at its center. His heart warmed when he saw children playing together.

Marylynn's expression fell. "Barnabas… He didn't make it. The night you disappeared was the last time I saw him. I thought that you were with him, so I—" Joren's foster mother couldn't hold back the sobs that tore through her. "I'm so happy you're here, Joren."

Joren had allowed himself to hope for his foster father's survival. That hope tumbled down into the marsh along with Marylynn's tears. Still, he held her until she had settled. "Come in, Joren." She grabbed Joren's hand and dragged him to the center of the crystal. The rest of his party followed, staying silent while he spoke to his foster mother.

"Is this it?" Joren asked, realizing just how many residents Malazar had taken. She nodded, and Joren's flames lit with fury.

However, Marylynn didn't back away. Instead, she gazed at the artifact on his arm. "It can't be," she said.

"Your son is the next reincarnation of the phoenix," the mage confirmed. Marylynn examined Joren's party for the first time. Her eyes landed on Lyra, and the rogue blushed.

"You know about the legend?" Joren asked his foster mother.

She nodded. "It's an old story. Your father shared it with me when we were first married. Over the years, I've heard different versions of it, but to find out that it's real…" Marylynn opened and closed her mouth, unsure what to say.

"Why didn't you tell me about it?" Joren asked. He thought of how useful that information would have been when he discovered the artifact.

"As if we could get you to sit still long enough to listen. You were an active boy who longed to work with his hands," she explained, holding his hands in her own. She studied his burn scars and hard-earned callouses.

"That sounds like him," Lyra commented, her smile bright and hopeful. Joren couldn't help but return her smile.

Noting Joren's positive reaction to Lyra, Marylynn placed

her hand over Fenria and asked, "What do you intend to do with it, Joren?"

The blacksmith paused, unable to come up with a good answer. *"The choice is yours, Joren,"* Fenria whispered.

The warrior looked at all the people who supported him, both old and new. The villagers had gathered around to listen to their conversation and whisper legends of heroes' past to one another.

Joren's thoughts collided, forming an answer—the only answer that he was willing to give. "I'm going to show Aelloria that the phoenix has been reborn."

Note from the Author

Dear Reader,

Thank you for embarking on this epic adventure with Joren and his friends, and for seeing through the end of this first installment of a grand saga. You have witnessed the beginnings of a transformation, the spark of a phoenix, and the ignition of a destiny that will shake Aelloria to its very core.

This Fall, brace yourselves for *"Genesis of the Phoenix Dawn"*, where the saga will continue to unfold. New perils and promises will be discovered, and where the destiny of our heroes will take even more unexpected turns.

As you close this book and look ahead to the next, please take a moment to leave a review on Amazon. Your words, your thoughts, your perspective - it all matters to me.

I also invite you to share your ideas for the future of Joren's journey. Together, we can shape the future of this story. This is not just my tale to tell, but ours to weave.

In this world of Aelloria, we are bound by the threads of

an epic fantasy, a true litRPG adventure that continues to unfold. And I am immensely grateful to have you alongside me on this incredible journey.

Joel Poe

To get emails about free book giveaways, early advanced reader book copies and announcements for upcoming sequels add your email to my list:

https://joelpoe.com/contact/

Joel Poe

Acknowledgments

To the readers and fans whose hearts pulse with the rhythm of fantastical worlds, who embrace adventure in its countless forms, who lose themselves in the pages of stories untold, thank you.

To the anime enthusiasts, with your unwavering love for vibrant characters and intricate plotlines that transcend the bounds of reality, thank you for your enduring passion.

To the videogame warriors, who valiantly traverse virtual lands and fight imaginary foes with real determination, your fervor keeps these realms alive.

And to the members of our vibrant fantasy community, with your insatiable curiosity, your love for the extraordinary, and your ability to see magic in the mundane, thank you.

Printed in Great Britain
by Amazon

40761730R00096